origins of the lighthouse

robert stewart

Copyright © 2020 Robert Stewart

All rights reserved.

ISBN: 978-1-8381272-2-0

"... what is last in the order of analysis seems to be first in the order of becoming."
- Aristotle, *The Nicomachean Ethics*

Origins of the lighthouse

Robert Stewart

circles

I

It is a long way out to the lighthouse and the slender width of the peninsula makes the way look delicately poised and dangerous. The difference between the surface of the sea on each side is disorienting: to the left, small waves flap and jostle, searching for a groundswell of force that the shallow depth of the water cannot summon; to the right, the water is stretched thin and unruffled, retreating into the estuary over the furled flats of silt.

David, eleven years-old, wearing a plain white T-shirt and jeans and wheeling a bicycle assembled by a strange man who lives in a caravan park, is determined to reach the lighthouse in spite of all obstacles. And everything seems like an obstacle: the sea that at any moment threatens to overwhelm the peninsula; the road that is sinking into its insecure foundations; the chuntering merchant ships, cutting closely – too closely – to the shore; even the odd-shaped couple sitting before him, eating sandwiches and talking. They all seem like an obstacle, like an impossible combination of numbers too complex to calculate.

"This is red onion," he overhears the couple say with a note of jilted expectation.

There is a pause.

"It'll repeat, you know."

David has never made it all the way out to the lighthouse. He has made several attempts. For each venture he has overcome at least one hurdle only to discover another. But he can feel his confidence growing, and, in proportion, he has crept steadily closer to his target. Each attempt requires planning and reflection to ensure he has learned from previous attempts: to get past the barking dog outside the heritage centre, he has learned to bring his bicycle; he has learned to wear Wellington boots in case he encounters the snake he once saw disappearing into the long grasses just before the peninsula begins; to overcome his fear that a monster wave might wash him into the sea, he has learned to keep his head down and not think about it.

He has only ever made it about a mile along the road. At this point the road gives out; or rather it has collapsed, and a long bunker filled with broken bits of concrete and sand seems to be the only way to proceed. It is frightening enough to think that if the land could no longer support a road, there is no reason it should support a human being, even one as young and agile as him. The grated orange fencing stretched between two wooden posts at the point where the road has collapsed heightens the sense of danger. There is no sign that says explicitly 'No access beyond this point!' but this message seems to be implicit. And the lack of any sign to identify the danger means it spirals out of control in his mind. Will he become bogged down in a sandy quagmire and sucked into the sea below? Is the surface spread delicately across a thin layer beneath which are deep waters populated by sharks, salt-water crocodiles and unimaginable monsters with hollow eyes and teeth blunted by too much contact with bone? He is old enough to recognise that this is probably unrealistic but sharks seem more adventurous than herring.

Standing at a safe distance from the heritage centre and close enough to eavesdrop on the couple munching through their lunch, David begins to contemplate all the obstacles that stand in his way. They mount rapidly, and taken as a whole, leave him feeling dispirited. Even small things, like the wind, a suspicious rustle in the grass, or a plume of smoke from the dockyards several miles along the coast, can leave him off-balance. More than ever, he feels like a lubberly giant prone to distraction about to begin life as a tightrope walker.

But David is determined to reach the lighthouse. His determination has increased with – or because of – his confidence. And on this day he is more determined than ever.

It is mid-August, a mere fortnight before the summer holidays end. This is more significant than it would be in any other year. David is eleven (soon to be twelve) and he is about to change school. He is about to graduate from primary school (a place for children) to a comprehensive school (a place for young adults). He is worried about this change. He has heard mainly unpleasant rumours about the school that vacuums up children from the small, mainly rural, communities of which his own primary school and village is an out-posted part.

The thought of a comprehensive education fills him with fear. Not the kind of fear he experienced when he caught sight of the snake or even when he was wiped out by a rolling wave and dragged under the water, out of breath, out of control and soaking up seawater like a crustacean. These kinds of fear were, though unpleasant at the time, compulsive, involving, even exhilarating. But the thought of secondary school stirs in him a slow-rising panic, sick-making and dull, which before now he has never really experienced. If left alone with nothing else to keep himself occupied, he can stare at objects vacantly, stricken by this particular strain of fear as it swells and circles inside him. Which is why this summer, regardless of the weather, he is always doing something; and why he is standing at the beginning of the peninsula, looking out at the lighthouse, and listening to a rudely cobbled couple talk about their indigestion.

"What's that?"

"Mould."

"*Mawled?*"

"Straight out of the packet."

"Did she not fetch eyes on it in the shopping trolley?"

"Well she has a cataract."

"Oh."

There is another pause.

"D'yer want a bit o' scotch egg?"

David is suddenly taken by a now-or-never moment. A will to reach the lighthouse rises up inside him so intense and powerful that he climbs on his bicycle. This, even at this early stage in his life, he recognises is better than the fear of an education. Recklessly, carelessly, like a drunk tossing away his troubles in an empty wine bottle, he rides out this momentum, panicked and afraid, but prepared to charge head-first into the snake-infested sandpits and dangers that he will no doubt face in the course of the next three miles. And grimly he pushes down on the pedals with the soles of his Wellington boots.

"I shouldn't have had that red onion."

II

"And how old are you?"
"Eleven ... nearly twelve."
"So you must be going up to secondary school this year? An education. Now there's something. I have to tell you, that I didn't much value mine. It's not so much that I was badly taught or that the things I learned weren't useful. But what I was taught and the ethos I picked up from my school jars with the way I think about things now. In some ways I wish I had been taught differently. In other ways perhaps not (learning by default is a form of education). What do you think you will learn at your new school?"
"Dunno ... they do phi in the first year."
"Yes, and I suppose that is an elementary lesson that anyone who wants to advance their understanding of mathematics must attend. And supposing you learn phi you will have put in place the foundations on which to base a whole edifice of mathematical learning. Armed with your understanding of circular geometry you will be able to extrapolate conclusions, tease out logical deductions and perform complex acts of

speculative reasoning based on informed and logically verifiable arguments. And with the same knowledge you will be able to enter centre stage on a construction site and make authoritative decisions about how best to apportion and manage projects, and about what should be done with the girders. Yes, yes, I can see it now … there you will be, hard-hatted standing at the centre of a circle of men making decisions about girders. They will all defer to you and your great mathematical brain, jam-packed with the convoluted calculations that make things possible."

"Well … I'm not very good at … with phi."

"No? Then something else maybe. What else do you think you will learn?"

"They use Bunsen burners. Sometimes in the first week."

"Aha, well there's something. And with your Bunsen burner plugged into the gas tap on your bench you will conduct experiments with the elements of the periodic table; and in order to conduct these experiments, you will have to learn the table and learn all the atomic numbers of the elements in the table as well as their properties. Over time you will come to know and understand these elements, and their valence. They will become so familiar to you that you will come to think of them as a natural extension of your own thoughts so that you can judge them intuitively. In time, you will be able to contribute to – or even oversee – the complex laboratory processes that underpin the pharmaceutical industry; you will be able to work for companies that harness and distribute energy in the most efficient way possible; you will be able to monitor and balance the delicate chemical protocols of waste management. Education strikes again ..."

"I've only used a Bunsen burner once."

"Yes?"

"I set fire to the gauze."

"Oh ... well, we could continue with this process of elimination, but why do I get the feeling that it would be a waste of time – for both of us? Let's not eye the biscuits politely – the fact is that your education is going to be a disaster. You clearly have no natural aptitude for anything, and while you might score passable marks in the course of the next ten years or so, they will only firm up a reputation for mediocrity. You will witness accolades conferred on your peers, excellence and achievement attained through motivation, drive, ambition. There will be children who win scholarships to universities, who gain unprecedented marks in exams, who outperform their rivals on the sports field, or who show inventiveness and creative flair in the arts or technology. But you will be dragging your heels, lacking the deeper reserves of energy or even the natural physique to really compete with the leaders of the pack. And while these other young and upwardly mobile achievers will become cut and fine members of the professional classes at the helm of national affairs, you will be an overshadowed officer, an agent, an unremarkable verb bridging a stellar subject en route to an exalted place in the firmament. Don't you think?"

"I don't know."

"Yes, well it's hard sleight the hand of time. But, on the other hand, it does no harm to send out an armada with more than one plan of attack. Perhaps that's what I could offer you: options. I could make you aware that there are different views from which to choose. That's all. Nothing more than that. Do you understand?"

"Like one thing or another thing?"

"Exactly. This will be our agreement: you will go to school; you will learn like anyone else, and we will see where that takes you. But here ... and now, you will let me offer you an alternative education that is, as you will discover, quite different from anything you will learn at your new school. Will you accept this agreement?"

"Yes."

"Okay then. Of course, it won't be easy, and, like any education, we must progress in stages. And of course, there is no single way to learn. To teach this particular branch of knowledge can involve any number of curricula, all of which differ wildly. It is like a disparate collection of pilgrims who all converge on a fixed point in a country from different directions. Some pupils would, for example, prefer to start by laying out first principles, and conclude from them a complete organon of knowledge; others would prefer to commit large chunks of information – stories, facts, statistics, points of view – to memory; still others would choose to assemble their education in pieces from the ground up, building upwards in a sort of bovine act of drudgery. But I will teach you in a different way; because this is the only way I can teach you.

I will teach you by example – by one simple example, because it is the only school book I have to hand."

III

Walking over the collapsed stretch of road feels a little like a tentative stroll around a volcanic crater. Where there should be concrete, there is sand. The terrain, clearly too infirm to support solid structures, almost disintegrates into the water. At its worst, the depth of the trench takes David down so far that his shoulders fall level with where the road surface would have been, and makes his journey look like the stages of evolution in reverse.

He looks at the marks left by the tyres of his bicycle, scared that the tyres might press too heavily on the sand and scupper the film of nearly solid substance that separates him from the surrounding water. He tries hard to spread his weight evenly, and he moves quickly over the surface of the sand, wary of how easily it might betray his sureness of foot.

His mind is concentrated and his knuckles are white from the ferocity with which he grips his bicycle's handlebars. But there are dangerous lapses of concentration, as if a cluster of inane thoughts are trying to derail his journey. He keeps experiencing the same image. He sees himself as an illustration in a children's textbook designed to profile the different strata of the natural world, from the ionosphere to the earth's core. Except the strata not immediately visible to the naked eye do not complement his place in the natural order.

Apart from the sharks and crocodiles a few metres under his feet, he envisages a race of diminutive, sharp-toothed creatures sitting on toadstools; and beneath that he envisages a stratum empty except for a compressed channel of hurricane-strength wind circumnavigating the globe at ferocious speed. Whatever it is that stays out of sight, above and below, it troubles him to think that it sees no purpose in his journey along the peninsula, or even that it does not share enough in common with him to know and understand the idea of purpose. His relation to the world around him is like a conversation of unintelligible croaks with an alien creature.

His grip on the situation and reluctance to succumb to the imaginary distractions makes him look embattled. He takes each step with the effort of an arctic explorer too jaded to brush the icicles from his beard as he stumbles deliriously towards the undiscovered. The only thing that keeps him going are the reserves of will, a sense that, however laboured, his journey is important.

He climbs up on the remaining stretch of road, the surface of which remains more or less intact. An eerie silence inhabits the space between his current position and the shoreline.

The silence is frightening; it confirms and reinforces his dislocation from everything he has known until now. Not only is he separated from his home, but also from its habits of life. He has not thought about this before, but he begins to wonder if anyone lives in the lighthouse, and, if they do, whether and in what way they are different. Perhaps they might, in the words of the strange man who supplied his bicycle, 'speak posh'. Or perhaps they are even more unusual. Perhaps they are Egyptians. Or even posh-speaking Egyptians. If there is anyone out there at all, he is convinced they are different in some way. Why else would they live at the end of a peninsula? Why else would this border-control of silence exist? If there were nothing foreign about the lighthouse, the way would be paved with familiarities, the heart-stopping headlines on newspaper boards, or Julian's 'free style' hairdressers, and he would have more than once caught the smell of chip fat or beer.

He stops briefly to take stock of his progress and think about this difference. He has heard people – his parents, other adults – say how things are different in London, and he thinks that it is perhaps this kind of difference he is about to encounter. The lighthouse, though it is south, is clearly not London. But it might partake of London in some way, as though either the character of London radiates outwards or lesser instantiations of the capital have been transplanted to other parts of the country. He thinks that he might be about to come face to face with a Londoner who acts as an ambassador to the Northern provinces. Maybe a hackney carriage is parked behind the lighthouse and inside a cab driver sits with his feet up at the top of its interior, rhubarbing loudly about the bad weather and using unfamiliar words like 'wotsnames'.

He walks in on himself at lunch with these idle thoughts. Feeling ashamed, he picks up his bicycle, and, with a look of scalding concentration, he moves along the road into the shadow of his curiosity.

The lighthouse, when he reaches it finally, is offset from the road, which bulldozes between large banks of sand. The builders of the lighthouse have cleared a way through the left sandbank, and erected the building on the edge of the slender beach that runs, like the hem of a skirt, around the peninsula.

Its girth strikes him first; it is much fatter than it looked from a distance, though it tapers slightly towards the top. The wall at its base looks solid and impenetrable, so firm in fact that the scratched and peeling paintwork is a cosmetic irrelevance. It almost looks more permanent and sure of its place than anything else surrounding; the ground is clearly infirm, and cannot be relied upon for anything; the sandbanks are compacted and sluggish but not immoveable; even the sea, though constant, is relaxed about its place in the cosmos. But the lighthouse could not belong anywhere else, and would not resign its post without a fight. It sticks out through the crusty ground like the tip of an axis spiking through the earth's core to a place on the other side of the world.

The impressed windows, or portholes, indicate the wall's thickness. They disappear into an unlit interior several feet from the exposed surface of the wall. The windows appear to correspond to each floor of the lighthouse, but placed at different points of its circumference. Each window is boarded-up and a flimsy gauze lends added protection against potential intruders.

He approaches the main entrance to the lighthouse. The door is at the top of four steps, the second of which has worn away over time, leaving a smoothed dip in the stone. The door is padlocked. David, standing on the top step, presses his ear to the door, listening for a beating heart. But the only thing he can sense is more silence, as if the interior transmits the gradual wilting away of noise.

He is already frustrated, particularly having come so far. Why anyone would want to board up the lighthouse, is beyond his reckoning. He tugs on the padlock and pushes hard on the door; but the door scarcely moves under the pressure he places on it. The window on the ground floor, which is almost exactly a hundred and eighty degrees from the main entrance, is just as inaccessible. He can just about see the protected window if he jumps, but the wall is impossible to scale, and even if he could, the window would prove a challenge to break.

Fingerprints of a similar frustration are evident in the form of graffiti, sprayed artlessly here and there. It even looks like someone has vented their frustration by throwing missiles at the window – the gauze has taken a battering and chippings of rock have accumulated around it.

David kicks the wall limply and then throws a casual glance over his shoulder to see if anyone saw him.

He spends some time just walking around the lighthouse, at an equal distance from the base of the wall. He does not look directly at the building. He keeps his head down, and eyes fixed on his feet. There is something strangely addictive, hypnotising even, about this activity. The lighthouse seems to be pulling at him, like he is a moon orbiting a planet. At first, he feels like an involuntary and inert object charmed by a conjuror; but the more laps he completes, the more he thinks that, like the moon, he exercises his own peculiar influence on the building, and that he and the lighthouse are, in some way, reaching out to each other, involved in a physical conversation.

This encircling of the building becomes a studied emulation of its shape; and each lap brings him closer to an appreciation of the building's architecture, as if he has assimilated the concept of a circle.

He continues like this until he notices something. A large object, visible only through the corner of his eye, and over the tip of long grasses to his right, breaks his concentration. He stops pacing, raising his head from its fixation with the ground, and looks out to the beach. The object is indistinguishable, bronze-coloured and looks a little like a large funnel, part-submerged in the sand and touching the sea's perimeter. Even from this distance, and based on a momentary observation, a single word enters his head: shipwreck.

His interest in the object increases as he finds a route from the lighthouse through the grasses and onto the beach. The tips of waves lap the object. If he were less intrigued by this new discovery, David might have the sense that he is being watched – no observers are visible, but the combined objects of his new surroundings seem to be straining not to pry.

The sand is fine, but wet and solid, which makes it easy to tread. Wind dislodges the surface granules and blows a sandstorm in miniature down the peninsula. David looks at the sodden piece of metal in the sand. It is obvious that part of the object is buried. The visible part provides only a fragmentary clue, from which he will have to deduce its full shape, dimensions and nature. It looks like a chimney or smokestack lying on its side, which, in his rush to draw conclusions, he sees immediately as the part of a ship. He circles the object once, looking at it from every angle. The smokestack is attached to something, but in its current arrangement, this doesn't look like a familiar piece of machinery – maritime or otherwise. It looks more like a growth or fungus that threatens to overgrow the whole sunken mystery, obscuring any trace of craftsmanship.

David crouches and peers into the cold and crabby interior. Rust, seaweed and the lumpen distortions of salt corrosion deface the object. The smokestack acts as an ear trumpet for the sound of the sea, and rasps a wiped-out counterpoint of drips, squelches and suckling barnacles. A steady drip of water falls into a small bed of seaweed; but coinciding with the impact of each droplet is a louder sound, flat and firm. He cannot work out from where this sound is coming; and why it is getting louder.

An eclipse of light behind him and the firm thud of a hand on his shoulder interrupt his investigations and push the pump in his chest to its limits.

"It's a ship," says a voice.

David stands up, turns on his heel, and steps back into the inhospitable front end (or back end) of the object into which he has been thoughtlessly inserting his brain box.

"Just in case that's what you were thinking – you were right. It's a ship. Mangled now, I know. But it's a ship all the same."

The man watches David closely. He is tall, broad-shouldered with a face as round as a plate. David, who is at this stage afraid of dying, is not yet comforted by the fact that the man's head looks like the moon.

"What's your name?"

"David."

The man holds out one of his paws.

"And how old are you?"

IV

"One of the things that strike me is how different people looked. I'll be blunt: they were less attractive. I suppose, in part, for economic reasons – the standard of living was not so high; the diet may very well have been another reason. But perhaps, in genetic terms, we were different. We were uglier. Less glamorous, less stylish. If I think about the kind of clothes – they were simple, plain, cheap. Yes, mainly cheap. Sometimes hand-made. Anyway we were uglier. And men were built differently. Big, bear-like beasts cultivated by and for manual labour. Perhaps I am exaggerating. My memory is more mischievous than it is reliable ... What were we talking about?"

"I don't know."

"...Ugliness. Yes, we were a lot uglier then. Sour-faced and lumpy. Bodies like porridge. Not that I thought about it. I suppose I didn't walk into my local village, glance at the local folk and say 'Oh me-oh my-oh, please pass me the puke bucket because I find you so physically repulsive.' No, it didn't happen that way. It was just the way things were. They were a people of puddings. Stolid, plain, and phlegmatic. People had thicker arms. Men and women. They both had big tree-trunk arms. And some, I remember, had huge hanging sacks of fat swaying about under their upper arms – like physiognomic shopping bags.

'I don't suppose anyone really minded their ugliness. They were probably unaware of it. I certainly don't think people passed the time of day, rubicund and convivial, only to retreat before a mirror in their little homes and think 'What on earth am I to do? They'll never put me on the front cover of Good Housekeeping." Or "If only I looked like Veronica Lake!' No, they didn't do that. I'm quite sure ... but anyway I am getting off the point. What was the point? Do you remember?"

"No."

"What I suppose I have been saying is that I lived in a community – full of ugly people, to be sure. Ugly people lumbering their broken faces about quite happily. At the time I am thinking of, I was a little older than you. I was a young man.

'I grew up on the outskirts of a village. There were four houses, two either side of a dirt track that petered out into an unpaved lane. The two houses opposite my house were farm buildings. As far as I could ever make out, the same family lived in the two houses – or at least they were custodians of both houses. But they only lived in one. Why it should have been a condition of their tenancy that they should only live in one of the two houses, I don't know. I mean, I would have lived in both, wouldn't you? An elderly couple lived next to our family. Their children had grown up. They had moved to the city.

'Most of my childhood I spent outside (even in the winter). There were several woods nearby. Several farms; the remains of a monastery. I explored all of these places. I came to know every conceivable route through the woods, and I could account for all the rabbit traps; I knew about ponds known only to local farmers, about routes through hayfields. And all these explorations and expeditions I undertook alone. That was a condition of my life as a child; I spent my time alone, wandering – sometimes for miles on end – with no-one to keep me company. For most of my childhood I had not been too concerned about this – when I was aware of it, if I was aware of it at all, I think I liked it. In fact, I even sought it out. But I suppose that by the tail end of my adolescence, I was beginning to get an uncomfortable and compensating feeling that I should be involved more with people, and even that I wanted to be involved with them. This coincided – as you will not yet be able to appreciate – with an interest in the opposite sex.

'But having spent so much time on my own as a child, and, therefore, being so unfamiliar with other people (including the opposite sex), I was not comfortable around them, and my adolescence was ..., well, ... luridly painful. I was once caught in the thick of a towelling fight in the boys changing room after a game of football. This, if you don't know, involves pointlessly and thoughtlessly whipping each other with wet towels. I was never comfortable getting changed with other boys, let alone charging through the showers without shame, wielding a wet towel like a mason and chain over the war cries of hormonal young men. I took part. But it left me red raw and trying hard not to look like I was about to cry, which, if I think about, is how I seemed to spend most of my teenage years.

'One weekend I walked all morning. Sometime late in the afternoon I realised that I had come so far that I would not make it home before dark. I was forced to catch a bus home. And that was how it all began. Because on the bus, perched two seats in front, was a girl. And it was at that point that I first began to appreciate that most of the people I knew were ugly. Because she wasn't. She was clean, slender and proportioned. There was no excess. No superfluous growth. She was like someone who never ate anything other than a moderate portion of choice vegetables.

'All the way back to my village I tried hard not to stare at her, though I lost out to a sort of dumb curiosity. I remember that I had caught a glimpse of her from the front when I had stepped onto the bus.

'She never looked around at me. She didn't seem to be interested in anything around her; whether that was through a sense of superiority or something, I don't know. After her mere presence on the bus, the most surprising thing to happen was this — she stood up to get off at my stop. I thought quickly — if she were getting off at my stop this meant that either she was visiting someone in the village or else she lived there (possibly she had just moved there). In either case, this meant that there was a good chance (the odds changed with the scenario) that I would see her again.

'I followed her off the bus at a distance. By the time the bus had deposited me on the pavement, the girl had already crossed the road. She was making for the lane that led to a field across which led to my home. I watched her for a moment. Her walk signalled composure. She was a paragon of presentation. It really was quite unusual. I mean, in the context of my village.

'I walked across the road. I followed her. I followed her down the track, and at a distance. The path went by the edge of a small brook, over a field left fallow, and through a small wood. All the time I kept thinking that she had been taught to walk by a master. She had spent hours from an early age walking up and down a hall balancing porcelain dining ware on her head. Her walk showed her education, maybe even a degree of privilege. I might have felt annoyed by her, were it not for the fact that it was all ... so unusual. I mean really — nothing like this had ever happened before.

'All the way down the track, along the bank of the brook and over the field, it had never occurred to me that she knew I was following her. I had not even thought about it. I must have assumed it. But as we entered the wood, she slowed down noticeably, so that the gap between us narrowed. She never looked around. She never so much as looked sideways. Not that I noticed anyway. Perhaps she heard me. It's possible.

'In the centre of the wood, she stopped. She stood still, head forward, fixed in the centre of the path, as stationary as any one of the trees. I suppose I should have kept going, but it was as she stopped that I suddenly had a very strong intuition that she knew I had been following her, and that she even knew I had been stealing glances at her on the bus. I went on slowly until I was only a few feet behind her. There, I stopped. She turned to face me.

'"What's your name" she asked

'I told her my name

'"You were on the bus, weren't you?"

'I told her I was.

'"I know you weren't following me … if that's what you were thinking. Is that what you were thinking?" she asked.

'I didn't say anything.

'"I know who you are, you see," she continued.

'I still didn't say anything.

'"I mean, I have seen you before," she explained.

'I forced a question.

'"Where?" I asked.

'She looked at me with well-practised confidence.

'"Here," she said.

'"I stammered something.

"'I've seen you here," she repeated – I remember she repeated this.

"'Here on this path?" I queried.

"'Well not here on this path exactly," she replied. "But I mean here ... more generally. Over there, more precisely" she said, pointing in the direction of my home, "out of my window."

"'Out of your window?" I repeated.

'I thought for a while.

"'Do you understand?" she asked.

"'I don't ... do you live ...?" I continued working through the options (it was beginning to dawn on me slowly).

"'Yes, I live in the house opposite. Well, I haven't been all my life (I think you would have noticed)." – she laughed at this – "No, you understand, I have just moved here. I have just moved to the countryside. The air is quite bracing. Don't you think the air is quite bracing?"

'I was still trying to take everything in.

"'You live opposite? In the farmhouse" I said.

"'Yes," she replied.

'I remember that I just stared at her blankly for a moment. Now that I think about it I suppose it must have been quite disconcerting for her. But I was so taken up with the whole situation – by the fact that she was standing before me in a country lane as plain as day, or even that she was there at all. And at times like this, it is easy to feel disassociated from reality.

"'Are you all right?" she asked, keeping a shadow of irritation out of public view. "Did you ... do you understand me?"

"'Yes,'" I said. "Yes, I understand you."

"'Well then,'" she went on, "you will understand that we are neighbours. Perhaps you would like to show me around. Not, I imagine, that there is a lot to see – sheep and that sort of thing."

"'Uh huh.'"

"'Farming here doesn't seem to be done very economically,'" she said. "I mean there aren't many machines."

"'I don't know,'" I said, shrugging. "I'm not a farmer."

"'They make a lot of noise,'" she went on. "Sheep, I mean."

'Her tone mellowed as I got to know her, but it was never very far from imperious observation.

"'They're not as noisy as a motor vehicle or a steam engine,'" I said.

"'Yes, that's true,'" she conceded, rocking effortlessly onto the back foot, "and they are nothing like as noisy as the city. There, you have cars, buses, trains, and besides that I suppose there is also the noise that comes from all the people. There are so many people in the city. Have you ever been to the city?"

"'No,'" I replied.

"'That's where I come from – the city. From London actually,'" she added, feigning an afterthought.

"'I didn't say anything. I wasn't sure what to say.

"'I'll only be here for a short time. My father – well, he is under great strain really; so, you see, my mother and I are … *mitigating* …'" – she had to search for the word – "... the strain. I suppose it's not right to go into all the details."

'"I had no idea what she meant so I stayed quiet.

'"You don't say very much ... *do you?*

'She added the question so that I might confess it publicly.

'"No," I said.

'"Can you read?" she asked suddenly.

'I blinked.

'"Yes," I replied.

'This seemed to reassure her.

'"That's good. Because there is nothing so important as education; and, of course, reading is an essential part of an education. I shudder at the intellectual under-achievement of ... well, never mind that. There are many inequities in today's society rectified only by those with the integrity and determination to act."

'This was the sort of thing she often said, and because I could never tell whether it was a lesson I was meant to digest or whether it was an invitation to discuss, I always kept quiet.

'She continued (she always continued).

'"Mrs Cowley said that you are a quiet boy. She said that you spend a lot of time alone. I suppose that's because you live in this very remote part of the countryside, yes? Well, I suppose it is. She said she thought you might be willing to talk to me, but that I should not be too upset if you were to remain taciturn and sullen. She said that boys are often sullen and taciturn, and that sometimes they are even like this as men. I'm taking it for granted that you know Mrs Cowley – the lady who rents the two houses opposite you."

'I nodded.

'"Well … do you mind talking to me or would you like to remain sullen and taciturn? I am sure we can make arrangements to avoid each other, if necessary."

'"No, I wouldn't want that," I said.

'She preened with pleasure.

'"Well perhaps we could walk home together? And perhaps tomorrow you could show me around?"

'I told her I thought I could.

V

David watches the man carefully. He looks, in particular, at the opening and closing of the man's mouth. It operates like a cartoon character – its two main states are either fully open or fully closed, and it scratches out intermediary stages in a hurried act of tweening.

The man talks at length and in detail, in a way to which David finds it hard to relate. The idea that someone can hold so many words in their head and send them out into the world so fluently is bewildering. David follows some of the words, carried along on the swell of a particular thought that catches his attention; but his mind drifts in and out of focus.

He is still partly recovering from the surprise appearance of the man; how exactly he had managed to creep up on him so discreetly, and where he had come from, David could not say. It is possible that the man is a Londoner but it seems unlikely; the accent, though David cannot quite place it, is not similar to the London accent he has heard on television or in films. But neither is it his local accent. The man speaks English, and speaks it clearly and cleanly – there is no bastardisation, or grammatical eccentricity to suggest he is foreign. The man's voice and his inflections do not seem to have a home. For a moment, David imagines that the man was born and grew up in the lighthouse, and taught himself to speak and read by studying television newsreaders or weathermen, broadcasting in the same well-educated but rootless intonation.

"Between here and there," says the man, referring to the shipwreck and the lighthouse, "there is a story to relate. And this story is the school book from which I would like you to study. I must tell it to you in parts of course, and you are free to analyse those parts (in fact, it would be good if you do analyse them). Boiling it down a little, and putting it plainly for the thin of thought, this story is the history of a single idea: and that idea is the idea of a lighthouse. No doubt you have heard of other lighthouses; no doubt, you have even studied lighthouses; no doubt you have painted primitive pictures of them and posted them on your classroom wall. But have you ever really got to the bottom of the matter? Have you ever grasped the *essential* idea? I doubt it. Because the essential idea is not widely known. And though it might seem like I am blowing my own trumpet, the reason it is not widely known is that it is mine and is tied to me and my personal experience.

"This lighthouse," continued the man, gesturing wildly, "is the first lighthouse, the original, the archetype on which all instances are based. In the course of the history of lighthouses, their popular meaning, function and purpose has transformed and changed, like many things, like for example many words. But there is an original meaning that I want to teach you, and it is this meaning that will form your education under my instruction."

The man continues to explain, laying out the ground before they start the lesson. Some questions occur to David: Why will the history of the lighthouse provide him with an education? How will this be different from anything else he has learned or will learn in school? If this is the first lighthouse, when was it built? These are the big questions, but occupying the space between these questions are dense pockets of lesser questions, like clouds of gnats at dusk. More than anything else, he wishes that the man would go slower, and not use so many long words or, at least, not cram so many words into his sentences. David feels mildly panicked by this detail, and while he thinks he can grasp the basic direction of his new education, he is worried that, by not keeping up with the detail, he will overlook crucial bits of information.

Rather than ask these questions, for the moment, he trusts that the man will answer some of them as he continues. But already David is clearing out space in his memory in which to store all the unanswered questions that accumulate.

The idea for the lighthouse, says the man, occurred to him over a period of time. It did not come to him in a moment of inspiration. It will be hard, in this sense, for David to understand the core idea, because it is, perhaps, something that a student can only grasp through experience.

"But I don't want you to think that this idea is beyond you," continued the man. "The story as I will relate it begins when I was not much older than you are now. And it was my ideas at that time – though I later developed them – out of which the idea for the lighthouse grew. And if I could think them back then, I see no reason why you should not understand them (or at least relate to them) now. The basic idea was a child's idea."

The man pauses for a moment to watch his pupil.

"Do you have any questions?" he asks.

David is slightly taken aback by the question. It is the first time he has felt like a pupil since his journey to the end of the peninsula. And the question reinforces all the anxieties he has been nurturing since the man first started talking. The man's question gives David the impression that he is being tested.

"No," David says.

"Because if you have any questions, you should ask them. What I have said to you so far – it makes sense?"

David hesitates.

"Yes."

"And what have I been saying?"

David hangs his head. Though he has a notion of the answer, he is sure there is a subtlety which escapes him.

"You were telling me about your lighthouse. It's an idea you had. When you were a bit older than I am now."

"And do you understand why I am telling you about the lighthouse?"

"It's a different kind of education you are trying to teach me."

"That's right. What do you think about that? Does it not strike you as a little odd?"

David looks at the ground and blushes.

The man presses further.

"I mean does it not seem a little strange to you that your education should consist of a story about a lighthouse?"

"I don't know" says David, still looking at his feet, "I haven't gone to secondary school yet. I haven't learned much. So, I don't know if it is or it isn't."

"What do you think a lighthouse does? What do you think is the idea?"

David squirms further, as though someone is turning his viscera on a spit.

"Don't they warn ships? Don't they tell them where the land is?"

"Do they? Is that what you think they do?"

"That's what I thought they did."

"What if people on the land want to see where the ship is? Would they not need some sort of powerful torch?"

"I suppose."
"So it could work both ways."
"Yes."
"Ships want to know where the land is and the land want to know where the ships are."
"That's right."
"Very practical."

A feeling of exultation is preparing to launch inside David; he can anticipate the soaring confidence as he flies over the treetops, cities, mountains and lakes of his ignorance and self-doubt.

"But it's completely wrong."
"What?"
"After all, I should know. I am the inventor."
David is deflated.

"Of course, I don't deny that lighthouses have the meaning you have given to them," the man continues, "not for one minute. No. Naturally ideas evolve and evolve beyond the scope and imagination of the original idea. I am sure there are many lighthouses whose sole purpose is to signal to ships. Of course, there will be other lighthouses, with other functions, equally remote from the original idea. All I am claiming is that these ideas are deviations. In fact I would say that the many different uses for lighthouses are, in some ways, a corruption of a much more personal, a more intimate idea. Someone, so to speak, saw my lighthouse and thought, 'I know we could use that as a way of signalling to ships, warning them, as a way of saving lives'.

'And I don't even deny that the corruption of my original idea is a bad thing. Quite possibly it is even better than the original idea. Who can argue with saving lives? But, however useful and benevolent this departure from the blueprint, it remains a departure, and there remains a blueprint."

David's eyes have widened. His stomach feels washed-out, and the adrenalin that had been pumping his body and mind seems wasted. Failure leaves him floundering without hope before his teacher. He has not excelled; he has not even passed. He has barely spelled his name correctly. If lighthouses don't signal to ships, what else has he misunderstood? Are cars and trains everything they at first seem? And houses? People? Families? Is there anything he has so far taken for granted that he can still trust? Are there other uses for mushy peas? The whole universe of knowledge he has built up in his eleven years has contracted to the first sub-atomic gurgle of life.

"As I said," continued the man, "the idea was a child's idea; it developed over time, but the shoots of the idea occurred when I was not much older than you are now. So, I must explain how the idea occurred to me, which means I must explain a little about my childhood. And things were quite different in my childhood – very different from the way they are now. One of the things that strike me is how different people looked. I'll be blunt: they were less attractive."

VI

"Her name was Isobel. She wouldn't give me the full name. I think it was double-barrelled, and she didn't want to overemphasise her social superiority. It was implicit enough.

'The day after I met her on the bus, she came to call on me.

'"I have come to call on Henry-Herbert," she said loudly to my mother.

'And it can't have been long after breakfast.

'I remember I appeared sheepishly from around the front door, crawling out of my damp little burrow to fulfil my promise to her.

'She was bored before she even got started. She was someone who exuded energy and impatience with everything. I knew from the beginning that there would never be enough to satisfy her curiosity and demands. I lived in ... well, a place not unlike this – slow, bucolic; a place that carries on at its own pace and emphatically not the adrenalin rush of metropolitan life.

'So, from the word go, I knew it was all futile – I was her plaything. It was obvious. It was obvious from her mannerisms, her inflections, her comportment, and her own barely contained conceit of the situation.

'I stood outside my house, looking at her. My shoulders, I imagine, were slumped. She stood before me, arms akimbo. She may even have been tapping one of her feet.

'"Well ...?" she said.

'"Well what?" I replied.

'"What are you going to show me?"

'The question was asked in the same way that termagant housewives treat their cuckolded husbands in public; calling on the world to look upon – and condemn – the deficiencies of their loved one. But one of the redeeming features of the countryside is that people come in short supply, and when matronly women seek to exert the full force of social judgement over their partners, generally it goes unnoticed. Her demands were, so to speak, answered only by the sound of a cow manuring a patch of grass.

'"What are you interested in?" I asked, buying a little room for manoeuvre.

'"My interests are many and varie ... var ... I have many interests. Why don't you name some highlights, and I'll select the most interesting," she returned, throwing the responsibility straight back in my face.

'"Highlights?" I replied, a little distant from my centre of gravity.

'Under the spotlight, I wasn't sure if I actually ever did anything in my spare time. The places I had been and the things I did for fun, I had never thought of as discrete events. They just were. Like a field of oilseed rape. Or an elbow.

'"Come on," she said.

'"Well," I said, "sometimes ..."

'"Yes?" she waited impatiently.

'"Sometimes ... well sometimes, Buz and me ... we stand underneath the bridge," I stammered, not really putting this activity in its proper context.

'She was frowning.

'"What bridge?"

'"The one at the bottom of the hill," I clarified.

'"You mean the one that runs over the stream?" she observed.

'"Yes," I confirmed, "we wear Wellington boots."

'The frown hadn't disappeared.

'"Who's Buz? Is that a person? Is he real?" she asked, spreading the frown further across her forehead.

'"His dad's a carpenter," I explained, "in the village."

'I could see she was shuffling thoughts about in her head.

'"And why do you stand underneath the bridge?" she asked.

'"For the eels," I explained, hoping this would put the matter to rest.

'"Eels?" she blurted in a sort of high-pitched screech.

'"Sometimes you can see eels underneath the bridge. When we were younger we tried to wee on them."

'Her jaw dropped.

'"We don't do that anymore," I added.

'She didn't say anything.

'"Just in case they're electric eels," I explained.

'This must have been one of the first occasions when I realised, very faintly, that my own enthusiasms were not necessarily cherished in quite the same way by everyone else. It was also one of the first occasions when I could begin to feel my words lose their purchase as I spoke.

'"I wasn't suggesting that we *should* do that," I said, trying to climb out of my freshly dug hole.

'She had retreated into silence, which could have easily been caused by shock.

'"Oh no?" she said.

'"No," I replied. "It was just a thought, that's all. I'm sure there are other things we could do."

'"What sort of things?" she asked a little warily, perhaps worried that these other activities might involve eels or urinating on something.

'My brain was working hard and fast, trying to eliminate other infeasible options. I figured that if she wasn't the kind of girl who liked watering eels, she probably wouldn't much care for the other "manly" activities with which I kept myself occupied at that time. Climbing hay bales was out, and by extension, jumping about in silage would only make the hole deeper; neither did I pin her as the sort of girl who liked climbing trees, hiding in hawthorn bushes or finding imaginative uses for privet.

'"I know where there are some flowers," I said.

'Flowers, at the time and from my point of view, sat squarely with femininity, and a sudden image of her swinging her arms gaily through a forest on a bed of bluebells seemed like the quickest and most accessible way to make up for my errors.

'"So do I," she said, pointing at a patch of snowdrops.

"'I mean, I know where there is a whole wood of flowers," I continued, trying to make this sound as delectable as possible.

"'I'm not interested in flowers," she said tartly, and then added just to wound, "no more than I am in eels. It is a falla ... it is falla ... people are often wrong when they think that women like flowers. I don't," she explained definitely just to smother the issue at birth and also to make it quite clear that she was a woman and not merely a girl.

"'Okay," I said.

"'But," she went on, after she had allowed enough time for her rejoinder to sting a little, "I do like woodland. Tell me about that."

"'Well," I stumbled forward, scanning my memory for discriminate characteristics, "it's private really. It's owned by a farmer or something, and sometimes he patrols the wood with a gun and a dog, looking out so that he can shoot people. There are some wooden bridges over a stream that the scouts built once. And there's a house ..."

'I remember she interrupted me here.

"'A house?" she asked.

"'Well more a shack. The roof has caved in now. No-one lives in it," I explained.

'She considered this for a moment.

"'Yes ... yes, that sounds more interesting," she said.

'The idea of visiting the wood and the shack at its centre so excited her that I tried to avoid saying anything else for fear that it might change her mood.

'I hurried back into my house, found a coat and returned to lead her to the wood.

'The wood could have been no more than a ten minute walk from the house. To get into it, you had to walk past a goat fastened by a chain to a stake in the centre of a small grazing meadow.

'"I won't go past the goat," she said emphatically. "I do not want to be skewered."

'"It won't hurt you," I said, though I had always been a little suspicious of the goat.

'(Generally speaking, I have always thought that goats aren't to be trusted.)

'"I don't care. I won't go near that goat!" she exclaimed.

'And I think she may have stamped her foot at that point.

'"There's no other way into the wood," I said, a faint beat of exasperation beginning to rise to the surface.

'The goat looked between us with a sort of dull curiosity as it continued to grind hard on the already hewn grasses.

'"I will not accept goats! No goats!" she said to the goat, staring sternly at it.

'The goat swallowed the grass.

'A mixture of panic and anger forced me to act eventually. I lowered my head and charged at her. I rolled my head into her stomach, grabbed her around her legs, and swung her onto my shoulders. She screamed. I ran across the meadow, her legs kicking in the air, and the goat's head followed us with the impassive interest of an observer at a game of tennis.

'She was not easily assuaged once I had deposited her on the far side of the meadow, and since she was starting to annoy me, I didn't try to assuage her. I simply strolled forward into the wood, as she effused demands and stamped her foot a lot.

'There were other incidents on the way into the wood, if I remember rightly. She didn't want to cross the bridge that led the way over a small brook. The bridge had been built by the scouts on one of their afternoon outdoor survival exercises, but it had since not survived very well and wobbled a little when you walked on it. This time, I didn't bother to help her across. I marched forward and waited for her to follow. I reasoned that either she had to face the obstacle of the bridge or the obstacle of the goat, and really didn't care which obstacle she preferred to overcome. I could hear her protesting in the distance as I carried on, but I was slowly learning to tune out this constant griping.

'She caught up with me only as I entered the clearing in which the now dilapidated shack stood. In its own way, this part of the wood was quite beautiful. It felt like a centre that called on the surrounding nature to support it. The remains of a log pile stood next to the shack, overshadowing a wide-open space dappled with a light from the gaps in the trees. The shack itself had two entrances, one of which – for no good reason – was padlocked. The other door had been kicked in. Inside the shack, the floor was covered with branches, leaves, the remains of some broken furniture, and miscellaneous rubbish left there at one time or another. There were, I seem to remember, sallow newspapers, an old oil lamp, and an empty bottle of Glenlivet that had been used as a candle, and down the sides of which streamed tallow tears.

'When I pulled my head out from the shack, I saw that Isobel was behind me, looking over my shoulder.

'"Isn't it wonderful," she said.

'And then she spent about ten minutes circling the shack, examining every spider web, and surveying it from every possible angle. Why it was so wonderful was mysterious to me (though I had always liked the shack) – in any case it was a relief to know that there was something in my mundane world that could stir in her such excitement.

'Finally, she perched on one of the upturned logs that the scouts fashioned as seats. She continued to stare at the shack.

'"This hut reminds me of my father," she said. "It reminds me in particular of a story that my father told me. It was a story about a man who lived in a hut."

'I asked if she would mind telling me the story her father had told her. She agreed. It was all about a man who decided to live on his own terms, so he retreated to a wood and built a house for himself.

'The man had been apprenticed to a farmer originally, and worked as a carpenter. But the farmer treated him badly, often degrading his work, and complaining about him in front of the other farm labourers. Though he found it demeaning, the carpenter could live with his overbearing employer. He learned to turn the other cheek.

'More than anything else the carpenter wanted to take some pride in his work. There had been many occasions where the farmer has asked the carpenter to repair joists and beams, or make improvements to the hay barn. The carpenter, who had considerable knowledge of his trade, treated these tasks as challenges, and he would often make innovative suggestions to the farmer on how improvements could be made. But the farmer always knocked back his suggestions – "Just fix it right," the farmer would say.

'The carpenter always did as he was asked, but his frustration grew. And an idea stoked his frustration. It had occurred to him that he was investing all his time in tasks dictated by the needs of the farmer; and even these tasks caused the farmer no real pleasure – he only needed the carpenter to accomplish them to ensure the continuing livelihood of the farm. No-one, it seemed, saw any merit in the carpenter's work. If, however, the carpenter found a quiet retreat in a forest somewhere, he could live off the fruits of the land and put all the many aspects of his skill and imagination to work on a house for himself. It would have to be simple – so more like a cabin or hut than a house – but he could nevertheless make it an exceptional piece of architecture. He could spend time over it to refine his ideas and produce a polished product. It would represent the sum total of his aspirations as a tradesman, something into which he could pour all his efforts and ideas, and something he could undertake for its own sake rather than for someone else's benefit.

'So, the carpenter retreated to a wood, and laboured over his hut, making sure that every truss and timber served the inspiration of his vision. The result was remarkable; he produced a dwelling unlike any other, one that was not recognisable in the architectural style of any other building of the region. It was altogether idiosyncratic, and closer to a work of art than a building.

'Though the cabin was in the centre of a wood, others soon learned about it, and news of the extraordinary building spread to the smallholdings and even the small villages and towns in the surrounding area. People came to visit and admire the building.

'The carpenter felt vindicated. Here was proof that it paid to pursue your own vision. He liked meeting his admirers, chatting to them in an unassuming and self-effacing way, but relishing any compliment they gave him.

'He felt established securely on his throne of innovation and expertise, until someone from one of the local villages brought a friend from outside the region to look at the cabin. The outsider was impressed by the carpenter's work, and he commented on how unusual and original the building was. The outsider said that it reminded him of a church he had visited in the West Country several years ago, whose unusual tracery and Byzantine beauty was widely regarded.

'The carpenter was shocked and a little put-out to discover a rival to his building. The outsider seemed to sense this, and, twisting the knife into the carpenter's pride, he added that though this church was spectacular, a cathedral in Spain boasted carpentry governed by a strange medieval doxology that hardly anyone could even begin to understand. The cathedral had been built over many years, according to a set of arcane principles based around sacred numerology.

'The carpenter looked visibly affronted. The outsider laughed, and went on to explain that, despite the exceptional genius of the Spanish cathedral, he had heard of buildings in India that used the grammatical system of its ancient scriptural language, Sanskrit, to create purposefully ambiguous and nuanced meanings illustrative of the complex and variegated centuries of people, culture, myth, religion and language. So much so that some people argued these buildings amounted to a physical representation of the one in the many, and an intimation of the invisible world through the visible.

'The carpenter was crestfallen. The outsider laughed again.

'"But what does that prove?" said the outsider.

'Naturally, this whole episode left the carpenter subdued. The revelations rippled across the previously placid surface of his self-esteem. With a few pieces of second-hand and unverified information, he had entered a much larger world. His achievements, which had until recently seemed immense, and maybe even unparalleled, were now dwarfed. Each time he returned to his cabin, he felt ashamed of it, angry with it, and angry with himself. His cabin probably looked ludicrous next to the Spanish cathedral or any of the Indian buildings. It was laughable, and if architectural experts – rather than ignorant common folk – were to cast their eyes over his cabin, they would find *him* laughable. He *was* laughable.

'He should, he decided, have remained under contract to the farmer, mending fences and building barns. Who in their right mind took up carpentry for its own sake?

'Now that he could see this, he would sometimes give his hut an irritable kick or punch, and where he had previously maintained the cabin assiduously and with affection, he could no longer find the motivation. Slowly it fell into disrepair, and acquired in the course of several years, a weathered and dilapidated appearance. Weeds started to grow up through the slats, a fungus began to grow on the outer walls, and the roof began to leak.

'The carpenter's appearance changed as well. He no longer bothered to shave or wash, and he wandered around the woodland smelling terrible and looking dishevelled.

'His anger at himself gradually subsided into a kind of mute ritual of subsistence; he would wander about the wood with a shotgun, hunting rabbits and game. And no-one came to see him or his cabin anymore.

'Things went on like this for the better part of his life – his cabin declining as he declined. It stayed this way until his sixty-fifth year. He was seated on the small veranda he had built so many years before, overgrown now with nettles, dock leaves, ragwort and other weeds, when he began laughing, a deep, visceral, and choking cackle. From where the laughter came or why it came, the carpenter didn't know (and by this stage, he didn't really care). But it didn't stop. He chuckled and rasped, a wheezy bark of laughter that caused his body to shudder. He would make strange noises, infected by the tonality of his laughter – "ooow-eee" he would say walking through the wood, or "yah-haaah".

'Slowly, a trickle of individuals returned to the wood, curious to know at what the man was laughing. But the more they returned, the more they just liked listening to his laughter.

'"You might think that I am strange," Isobel said to me once she had finished telling this story, "but I always find that story comforting. I think this must be because my father told it to me; and each time I remember the story, I can hear his voice in my head."

'I looked at her, aware of how much her mood had changed since she had seen the old hut and told me the story.

'"What's happened to your father?" I asked eventually.

'She stared at the hut pensively.

'"He has gone away," she said."

VII

The introduction of a woman is, for David, more of a distraction than a device that sheds light usefully on the purpose of his 'education'. He has not had much experience of women, and he is young enough to have only a slender appreciation of the differences between the sexes. His only real understanding of female sexuality is a caricature of the truth, derived from black and white movies. Breasts, in these pictures, are hard to ignore, and they assume larger-than-life proportions in the impressions they leave on the eye of the mind.

None of the women he knows have breasts like this, but he is happily unaware of this fundamental disparity between the images broadcast on the screen and the handful of women in his life. The women he sees on television are, he imagines, the women who live elsewhere in the country, and also the women he will necessarily meet in later life. He imagines these women steering their pyramidal boobs down the passageways of buses and trains, and making clumsy manoeuvres down the aisles of supermarkets; he sees rows of protuberant chestiness in open-plan offices, all distended to the same length and moulded to the same proportions, like a mass collection of radio transmitters broadcasting the party line.

He knows girls his own age, and he knows middle-aged women. But the female demographic in his region includes hardly anyone between these ages. Girls simply leave when they get to a certain age, which is an indication of the kind of life that goes on in his community, and even the wider region. Where they go is not something he has really thought about until now. Where could they go? Lincolnshire? It seems unlikely. He is not sure of this, and he has no concrete evidence one way or the other, but he thinks they might descend on one of many cities, or spend their lives migrating between the heady atmospheres of different cities. He knows one girl who migrated to Denver.

He can only think of one woman younger than middle age and older than him. She works in the heritage centre at the foot of the peninsula; she appears from time to time in fleece, smelling of cigarettes, and guides cars to a suitable parking place on the chipped macadam. The rest of the time she spends behind a desk in the centre, sometimes with a boy, but often alone.

This leaves David with very little raw material on which to base an understanding of how the history of lighthouses might relate to women. Even in the most tenuous associations, he struggles to see how the man's encounter with a pretty girl could lead him to the invention of a lighthouse. The connection is far from seamless in his mind, which, he thinks, is another poor reflection on his innate intelligence. A nimble mind or a lateral mind would have seen the connection immediately, and would now have a clear idea of where the man was leading him. But the man is only compounding his confusion by talking about women. Already he can feel a peculiar mixture of ingredients coalescing in his head, and he has a sinking feeling that, in the final analysis, it has something to do with breasts and modern architecture. And is that really any substitute for a comprehensive education? He doubts it. He is starting to think that he is just a victim of another deranged adult life.

Part of David wants to call things to a halt, to take some time out just so he can consolidate the things he has learned so far. This was not the way he had imagined his education, and it is very different from the primary education he has experienced until now.

He has, of course, been in an educational jam before. He is not complacent about his intelligence, but often finds that he has to compensate for lapses of concentration by reading between the lines or relying on logical guesswork. In one crucial lesson when he has was seven, his teacher explained the difference between vowels and consonants; David had not paid attention, thinking instead about the time a girl had drawn the curtain on the boys changing area to expose him in his y-fronts (the humiliation was still hot). The teacher caught him out by pointing to successive letters of the alphabet, and asking him to say whether they were consonants or vowels. He had assumed that there would be some pattern, and started with an alternate pattern. The teacher soon tired of his failure to substitute logic for learning and explained the idea to him again.

This was among his first experiences of failure; but it did not galvanise any will to do better. It weighed around his neck and did not go away. And each failure that followed only added to this weight. Education, in his experience, is not constructive or liberating, but a recurrent illustration of his inadequacy and a gradual erosion of his esteem.

The sudden profusion of lessons with which he is now faced is confusing and feels more like a nail through the heart, or an act of intellectual euthanasia. Like a cornered animal, he is flitting around frantically, looking for a way to mount a counterattack and restore his dwindling pride. But it is hopeless. It feels like the man is unfairly piling on him material beyond the aptitude of even an able student. There are now so many questions in his mind that he cannot remember them, and so many variables in the equation he is trying to solve that his head hurts. He is reaching the point where he knows he can't go on; and no other course of action is left except to curl up and die.

The man seems to be studying David. He has stopped speaking and is looking intently, searching for signs and symbols open to some kind of interpretation.

David waits, his heart pounding, his legs shaking. He is torn between a wish that he had never ventured out to the lighthouse, and an even more horrible feeling that if there is no hope out here, then there is simply no hope.

"Do I frighten you?" asks the man eventually.

"No," David replies weakly.

"Are you saying that because you think that's what I want to hear?"

David swallows air.

"No."

"And you understand everything that I have been saying?"

David shuffles about and sniffs.

"Yes."

"It all makes sense?"

"Uh huh."

"Then what do you think is the point of our meeting?"

"I thought ... I thought it was the light..."

"... I don't mean that. I mean if it is all crystal clear to you, then surely there is nothing left to teach you?"

"Well ..."

"Do you know what the word 'physiognomic' means?"

"I'm sorry?"

"'Physiognomic' – do you know what it means?"

David swallows hard.

"I ... no ..."

"I used that word ... not so long ago. But you don't know what it means. Perhaps its meaning is relevant to the things I have been saying? Why else would I use the word? For fun? Do you think I used it for fun?"

"No."

"And do you think that if I asked you to repeat the story I have started to tell, you could do it? Could you recall from memory all the dialogue?"

"Well ... no ..."

"Word for word?"

"No."

"And if I asked you to tell it to me next week – I guess you would find it even harder?"

"Yes."

"Well then ... it has been thirty years since these events happened to me. Does that not make you a little bit curious? Do you think that every word I hear is seared into my memory forever?"

"I don't know."

"But it seems unlikely, doesn't it?"

"Yes."

"So, I would say you have been lying to me. I would say that you do have problems with the things I have been saying. I would say that you don't understand what I have been teaching you, why I am telling you a story from my childhood, how that relates to the story of the lighthouse, and why I am even telling you about the lighthouse. To stretch it out a little further, I would say that it is pretty unusual – maybe even a little improper – for an old man to ambush a young boy and persuade him to undertake an alternative to his secondary education. Hardly normal behaviour.

'I would say that you have been frightened since you first caught sight of me. I would say that you are struggling to keep up with everything I have been saying, and that you don't understand what on earth I have been talking about. I would say you are nodding your head, and scrambling about in the dark in a desperate effort to keep me happy (like you try to keep all your teachers happy) so that at some point you can relax, you can escape, you can, at last be free from all the pressures that your incipient little life is only just beginning to sense. But the irony is that you only travelled these three miles to the end of the peninsula because you saw *that* as an escape. And instead, what do you find at the end of the peninsula? You find just another version of the thing you want to avoid before you have encountered it. No fresh air. No freedom. Just another warped human being trying to persuade you that their words will ensure your preferment in the world. It must be a disappointment.

'Your approach to education is like the blunt responses you have given me so far: an act of wild-eyed repulsion. All your intelligence must go into understanding something in order get it out of the way, in order to evade it.

'But, you see, I will not waste my time on an education that you will bat back at me in order to run off to another part of the world where you can be alone. And I will not be a disappointment to you. So, for these reasons, I want to hear you say something. Do you know what I want to hear you say?"

"No."

The man leans over David so that he is close enough to ensure his words enter David's ears without being carried off on the wind.

"I want you to say these words: 'Are you just making this up?'"

"'Are you just making this up?'" David repeats thoughtlessly.

"That's it. Those are the words. Now you have to say them. You have to speak them."

David looks at the round face of the man. He can feel a smile burgeoning inside him to mirror the smile on the face of the moon that meets him.

"*Are* you just making this up?" he asks the man.

The man stands up straight again with a sense that he has accomplished his mission.

"Let me see – where did I get to? One afternoon on the bus. First meeting on the field. Yes, that's how it happened. She left quite an impression. I certainly won't ever forget her. It would be hard to forget her, even if you didn't know anything about her. Like her name. Though I did know that. Her name was Isobel. She wouldn't give me the full name. I think it was double-barrelled, and she didn't want to overemphasise her social superiority. It was implicit enough."

VIII

"We visited the hut many times. I came to rely on it. It was my cure for everything. If she showed even the slightest sign of her hot temper or general demanding character, the shack was always the answer. It was my panacea.

'Most of the time I found her maddening. She seemed to take every opportunity to make me look ignorant and simple. She flaunted her sophistication, her upbringing, her intelligence, throwing at me arguments, social comment, and observations that would never have occurred to me. She was the authority on everything, from why trains stopped running when it got too hot, to the most appropriate attire for a Saturday out in the town. Whether any of her accumulated knowledge had any ground to it, I never knew. And in a sense it didn't matter. She had been brought up to rule, and decree. Her education taught her how to *appear* authoritative. It may sound cruel, but she was like a well-bred animal designed to serve a particular role in society. Her character had been carefully hewn to fulfil that role.

'Most of her talk and superiority left me silent. I did not have the education, the knowledge or the natural intelligence to respond. She was cleverer than me.

And, like an aristocrat sharing a happy relationship with her estate workers, she looked on me as some sort of farmhand or gamekeeper, good for nothing but manual labour. If ever I made an observation or, worse still, referred to a book I had read, she just ignored it. She did art, reason, culture. She made it plain. She said she was going to study English Literature at Cambridge University.

'On one occasion, she was talking about food. I don't remember in what context. Perhaps it was a restaurant she had been to recently. She mentioned yoghurt. At the time, I had never heard of yoghurt.

'"What's yogurt?" I asked her.

'She paused for a long time, and then, as though I had offended her mortal being, she stopped and stared at me with pincer-like eyes of disbelief.

"What do you mean what's yogurt? You mean you don't know what yogurt is. Henry-Herbert, what kind of a person are you? *Everyone* knows what yogurt is. What kind of person are you Henry-Herbert? Dear me."

'I remember I went home and asked my mother. She didn't know either. I only found out in the 1960s.

'She was the first person I have ever hated, and also the first girl to whom I was attracted. For a long time whenever I thought of her, I felt a kind of choking silence, born out of a situation to which I never really knew how to respond. But also ... I thought she was very desirable. Physically, I mean. And I wanted to communicate with her from some place other than on the receiving end of her abuse. I wanted to mellow her; to make her into something likeable as well as desirable. And that's why we often ended up at the shack in the wood. Because it mellowed her.

'And it mellowed her because it reminded her of her father. This was the key. The key to her soft underbelly was her father. So, I explained my theory to her.

'I chose my moment, at the end of an afternoon we had spent together in the wood. She was sitting on one of the upturned logs as I lay in the long grasses, half-glancing at her legs.

'"Did you know that the earth is round?" I asked.

'"Yerrss," she replied.

'She became more sardonic when she was relaxed.

'"But if you think about it, we think in straight lines. If I walk across the field, I begin at one place and end up in another. But if the world is round, this means I am walking over a very small fraction of its surface. And in theory if I kept on walking, I would end up back where I started from."

'She sighed.

'"What are you talking about Henry-Herbert?"

'I persevered.

'"Well what if other things that appear straight are in fact circular. Lives seem to begin at one point and end at another. Football matches start at zero minutes and end at ninety minutes. Books have a first page and a last page. But what if all these are just a part of the circle, so that at some point, all football matches begin again and all books start over. Maybe everything is on a loop. And maybe all thoughts are like that too. They see a fraction of the surface that gives the impression of progress from ignorance to knowledge, but in reality all knowledge is turning back into ignorance and vice versa. So, in reality nobody really knows what's what."

'She thought for a moment.

'"You have some strange ideas, Sonny."

'But I could tell she was interested. Or at least curious.

'"It's only strange because it's counter-intuitive," I said – except I wouldn't have used the word counter-intuitive at that age. "I mean if you think about it, there are lots of things that aren't what they seem. The sun looks closer than it really is. Sticks look bent in water. Why should everything else be different? Maybe circles are a better model to follow. And it might not be a bad thing. It means all the good things will come around again."

'"It also means that all the bad things will as well," she jumped in.

'"But neither has the edge," I retorted, "and it means that you always have something to look forward to. And that if you didn't savour the moment the first time round, maybe you will the second. You and I could be talking like this again somehow in some place. Perhaps there will be differences. Perhaps it will be a different time, and a different place. But the time will come again."

'She smiled.

'"And it would mean that all the people you have left behind – I'm not saying died necessarily though it could apply to them too – you will see again. Like your father for example. You would see him again."

'"Who says that I won't see him again, anyway?" she said.

'I didn't say anything.

'"But it's a nice idea," she said eventually. "I like it. But I mean, how would it work? We couldn't have this conversation again, saying these exact words?"

'"I don't know," I replied, struggling to work this out, "it's just the image of the world that made me think about it. And the idea of lots of different people all over the world occupying a particular bit of it and using the space they occupy to create their understanding of things, when in fact the world is much larger; and if they explored the larger world, they would end up returning back where they began."

'"It might be a bit of a disappointment," she suggested.

'"Or you might see it again in a different way," I countered, trying to grasp this idea.

'But I had gone far enough. A dreamy expression melted the harsh angles of her face.

'"I suppose I would see things in a different way," she said, like me, thinking out loud, "because you would have also spent so much time away from the things you know, and you would be thinking about what you know, aware of all the things you didn't know before."

'"It could be very depressing," I ventured.

'"Or it could make you appreciate them even more; because you might see them for what they are. How would you react if you saw me again?"

'My emotions were too conflicted to answer that question honestly, so I said I would probably ask her around for some jam roly-poly.

'I didn't want to ask her how she would react to a re-encounter with me, so I asked a different question.

'"What would you do, if you saw your father again?" I asked, partly out of genuine curiosity.

'She thought about this, clearly excited and pleased by the question. She looked at me. She leaned over, folding her arms into her stomach, and kissed me on the cheek."

Robert Stewart

darkness

I

The sun bursts through a cerulean sky. A gentle breeze rustles the sedges as seamlessly as the movement of a snake. The car park outside the heritage centre is empty, and the centre seems to be closed. David can usually spy the head of the girl who runs the centre; her scalp appears above the desk behind which she sits reading about celebrity gossip in-between her duty to the nature reserve. The only sign of life is the motorbike that belongs to the boy with whom David has seen the girl several times.

The day is almost unnaturally bright, and the sea uncharacteristically blue. The lighthouse, at the end of the peninsula, stands crisply and clearly as though it has just returned fresh from a professional photoshoot, and is soon to appear on the front cover of National Geographic. The air feels clean, for once transporting the salty chill of the sea rather than the pollutants and industrial smog from a few miles along the estuary.

Where the slender waif of land usually invites wildlife into its protective fold, the sun and the gentle breeze tempt birds into the open. Grebes and oystercatchers explore the fertile plains of mud, and gulls hop about in private corners of the beach.

Unlike the last time he journeyed out to the lighthouse, there is no-one in sight at all, which is unusual considering the weather. If the centre is closed, he is not sure why. Perhaps the peninsula is not a place to visit on sunny days; those who feel inclined to visit the coast on days like this are more likely to visit one of the established coastal resorts. The peninsula is too austere and bleak for a windbreak, and bucket and spade.

He hesitates once again, but for different reasons. It is no longer the unknown that creates the psychological barrier. If anything it is the opposite. He has found his thoughts returning again and again to the man who lives in the lighthouse, and his memory of that first experience sits like an ulcer in his stomach, transmitting hot spasms of discomfort. In the company of overwhelming isolation, he is not sure he wants to meet anyone, including the man. The man, like many adults he has encountered, fills him with panic and fear. Instead, he only wants to be alone with his thoughts, the birds, the sea, and a future that stretches out before him like the beach, untrammelled by the imprint of human feet.

Rather than an exploration of the unknown, his visit to the lighthouse is now governed by a set of expectations that turn on his all-important education. He is not travelling along the peninsula because he wants to, but out of compulsion or a strange, unfathomable obligation to the man, the bind of which is more elusive than an education dictated by government statute. If he were feeling rebellious, he might not go back to the lighthouse; he might find another isolated spot to explore. But there is something so extraordinary about the man's claims that jar with everything David has so far come to expect; this creates a glimmer of curiosity that makes him want to return. And something suggests to David that the man might carry him to the far side of his panic and fear.

He has not said anything to anyone – least of all his parents – about his last journey to the lighthouse. His parents have never told him that he should not travel out to the lighthouse, but he thinks he can second-guess their views. If he asked them, he is sure they would invoke a particularly gruelling story about life-threatening amphibious creatures or unexploded Second World War bombs to justify their prohibition. At eleven, he has learned only to ask permission when confident of a favourable response. In this case, he realises that it is safer just to keep quiet.

This is especially so now that there is a man living at the end of the peninsula. His education, however embryonic, has impressed upon him that he should cultivate a fear of strange men in remote places. He knows, almost intuitively, that he must not get distracted by a bag of sweets or the promise of a free ride to a theme park. These innocent flowers shelter only insidious serpents. So, if he told his parents about the journey he is going to undertake, they would go puce-coloured barmy.

But his equally embryonic judgement tells him that the man at the end of the peninsula has not stepped out of a five-minute educational horror film about the perils of park benches. The man is not offering David candy floss. He is offering him an education. David reasons that it is a condition of the chilling crimes perpetrated by men who loiter around playgrounds that they are preceded by something nice. Education emphatically does not meet this condition.

The odd behaviour of the man in the lighthouse, combined with the sense of obligation he feels towards the man, means that the issue is in no real doubt. He has come to the foot of the peninsula with every intention of continuing with his education; he will not turn back now.

And yet it is such a prepossessing day; one that was not designed for concentration and the pursuit of learning. The weather lends itself naturally to his real ambitions: exploration and adventure. One of the attractions of life on the coast is that there are so many places to explore, so many old buildings filled with faded wallpaper and the meditative click of a record player that has come to the end of a ballad as a pensioner sleeps in a Queen Anne armchair. It is easier and more liberating to be an impersonal observer of things than a pupil squirming uncomfortably under the weight of apparent stupidity.

David swings his Wellington boots over the frame of his bicycle and sets off down the bumpy track that leads to the man's home. He keeps his head down and pushes hard on the pedals, pumping up a momentum that will allow him to change gear, and coast at high speed towards his destination.

He reaches the collapsed stretch of road in no time at all, and comes to an abrupt halt, nearly somersaulting the handlebars of his bicycle in the process. He knows that he must dismount at this point, and wheel his bike through the sand until the road re-emerges intact.

He descends into the sandpit with caution; despite his safe journey out to the lighthouse and back only a few days ago, he still doesn't trust this part of the road. Not least because it has already betrayed the confidence of the concrete which it once supported. It strikes a particular nerve with him, because it seems to represent the shape-shifting and fundamentally duplicitous nature of the peninsula. The land might appear to serve as a bed for roads, or a home for wildlife, or a firm foundation for a lighthouse, but it is changing all the time.

David tiptoes over the sand with chased eyes and a slack jaw, like prey conscious of a lurking predator. To his alarm something catches his attention through the corner of his eye, which at first looks like a carnivorous animal moving furtively through the long grasses. David stops everything: his bicycle, his feet, his arms, his breathing – only his heart won't pipe down. Sweat begins to bead on his forehead.

On examination, the 'animal' appears to be moving; but it does not follow the meat-seeking trajectory of a natural born killer. It is moving vertically, up and down. Neither does it look like any animal he has seen in the countryside, in a book or in the quietly spoken programmes on television. He consults a mental taxonomy of wildlife, trying to match characteristics of this creature to the documented animals of the world; but it doesn't match. Instead it wobbles, like a jelly or a tranche of pork fat.

David tilts his head to one side, thinking that fresh perspective might clarify things. At this point, he discerns a clue: a crack that separates two large loaves of wonderfully white flesh.

"It's a bottom," he gasps.

This first encounter with the mysterious art of mooning brings a smile to his face, and for several long moments, he just stares happily at the bouncing buttocks, revelling in the privacy of his amusement. He has no sense, at this stage, of his involvement in the scene or that the buttocks might become conscious that they are being observed. But they appear to be so absorbed with their current preoccupation that it would take a calculated interruption to distract them.

David's amusement begins to fade. He continues to watch the buttocks, but more in the spirit of empiricism and the self-improving ambitions of an autodidact than a schoolboy fairly tickled by the sight of a bare behind. If he watches carefully, there are hints of frustration and discomfort. Far from self-possessed, the buttocks struggle with an impatient urgency, like a fat person trying to balance on a beach ball. The movements are not constant and rhythmical, but faltering and disjointed. The discernible flab on each cheek shakes, and makes the buttocks' enterprise look all the more laboured and inefficient.

David, who is dimly aware of what and who is involved, still finds interest in imagining the situation solely as it appears. From where he stands, the bodies underneath are concealed by the grasses, and the buttocks rise up, like the shaved head of a monk, out of the bushy undergrowth. Inactive they might be construed as a pair of large mushrooms or some other cleft species of fungus. But active they look like a new species altogether, a flightless puffy-billed bird made in the mould of the human derrière, a creature that hitched a lift on an industrial tanker from the South Pacific and jumped ship at the mouth of the river in order to find a favourable habitat to thrive and reproduce. Soon the peninsula might be filled with bottom-shaped birds, jouncing up and down, and making strange warbling noises.

There is something sad and almost pitiful about the buttocks considered in this way. They look like a misshapen creature bred for an illegal sporting activity or burdened with the effects of genetic aberration. If the buttocks had eyes, David imagines that they would stare at him with a mixture of abandonment and despair.

David catches himself coming close to feeling sorry for the buttocks, and realises that, not for the first time, he is letting his imagination run away with him. The peninsula is a haven for trickery, and the buttocks are no exception. On the surface peaceful and isolated, the crooked brush stroke of land conceals many hidden creatures. But already he realises that it is not a simple case of peeling away the layers of its appearance; because the layers that lie underneath are no less solipsistic.

Even so, David must get beyond the copulating couple if he is to make his appointment with the moon-faced man in the lighthouse. He doesn't want to give the couple the impression that he has seen them (and particularly doesn't want them to know he has been studying the top bottom). So, he decides to walk by nonchalantly, wheeling his bike. He whistles loudly to make his unassuming air quite clear. He thinks he can see the girl from the heritage centre trying to keep her exercised lover quiet while David passes.

David doesn't look again. He climbs onto his bicycle, sets off towards the lighthouse, still whistling a tune he once heard in a film. Its title, though he can't remember the lyrics, is 'Moon River'.

II

"When I was a young man, I got a job as a junior librarian at the Courtauld Institute. I moved into a small flat in Camden Town, which at the time was not an especially desirable place to live. It had a feeling of Victorian England. You felt like deformed excuses for human beings might stroll around any corner.

'The owner of my flat lived on the floor beneath me, and appeared outside my door from time to time. He never wanted to inspect the state of the flat, and he was never particularly concerned about whether or not I paid the rent. He just wanted to talk ... I remember I once asked him what he did for a living. He sort of shrugged me off and said carelessly that he did a spot of administrative work for the metropolitan police. He was also very affected, and when I told him – believe me, it was a mistake – that I worked at the Courtauld Institute, he went into raptures.

'I didn't know anyone. There is a sense in London that you are always only a discreet whisper away from the centre of things. And it is easy to feel charged by this expectation. Walk around one corner and you might descend to a sub-street-level party populated by narcotic-fuelled fashionistas at the cutting edge of popular culture. Walk out onto someone's roof balcony and you might find yourself talking to a permanent secretary at the Department of Health, an avant-garde émigré film director, or the Archbishop of Canterbury.

'Not that anything like that happened to me. I didn't know anyone, so I never walked into any parties. Even pubs and bars scared me. I would sometimes read the newspaper in a café. But that's not the point. The point is that, however misleading, the city gives out the impression that you are closer to the beating heart of civilised existence than you would otherwise be in the provinces or even in the suburbs. It was exciting. Yes, it was.

'Even I could see that it was exciting, and I lived the most nondescript life imaginable. I did a lot of walking, even through the trench-coat parts of Soho. I once walked from Camden to Kensington via Hyde Park, and most of the way back again. I didn't stop to admire buildings or pass the time of day with anyone (or if I did, it happened very rarely). Sometimes I would sit in parks. And sometimes I would meet one of the fellow librarians for a pub lunch on a Sunday, or we would go to the National Film Theatre to watch one of the films by Ingmar Bergman or Akira Kurosawa.

'But most of the time – certainly for the better part of a year – I was alone. You might get the impression that I was the sort of person who sat plaintively in parks, feeding the pigeons. But I wasn't. Though in my time in the metropolis I seemed to drift further and further into a state of unhappiness, in a way that I was not always fully aware of. It crept up on me.

'Up in Holborn there was an eatery – it was one of those old wartime places. Possibly it had been a soup kitchen. I would often go there for an evening meal. You would sit between stations, partitioned by slats of frosted glass, and a permanent fog of smoke clung to the ceiling ..."

"What was it called?"

"What was its name? The Bullfinch. Yes, The Bullfinch. But I think everyone just called it The Hatch because the waitresses picked up all the food through a small hatch in the wall at the back of the café. That hole in the wall was like a vision through the rood screen to the sacred rituals of the kitchen.

'It was here that I met this girl that I have been telling you about – Isobel – for the second time. We were, of course, older by this time. I must have been ... what? ... twenty four or five. I had not really kept in touch with her since we met in our teens. She only stayed in the house opposite mine for that summer, and then she moved away. She left no forwarding address. I expect she was glad to get away.

'Meeting her for the second time was a little awkward. Because I think the pair of us fetched eyes on each other in a state of semi-recognition. I remember I saw her first. I looked up from reading the paper as she walked into the café. I squinted at her, registering the fact that I knew her from somewhere. When I twigged who I thought it was, I decided to go up to the counter for a cup of tea to get a better look.

'Anyway, it was all a little ... awkward. Eventually we both realised that we knew each other, however dimly and distantly.

'We sat down together at my table. I felt like the interest I had expressed in her was more perfunctory than sincere. From the off, our second meeting was conditioned by the first. We were both withdrawn and maybe a little embarrassed around each other. I think because we were both conscious of our earlier selves, as though we were each a mirror in which the other could see hideous blemishes of character.

'At first I thought that our conversation would amount to no more than a bit of flummery. We chatted for a while. The balance of words had not really changed despite our change of age. She poured forth facts, anecdotes, snippets of information about her life in London, her time at Cambridge, even a brief time she had spent in Italy. But her mind seemed to operate at two levels: behind the pleasantries it felt like she was studying me, picking up signals, looking for some clue from which she could deduce a suitable judgement.

'"So, you haven't been in London for long, then?"

'"No, about a year."

'"Do you mind if I ask you something?"

'"No, go ahead."

'"Do you have many friends? It's just I have the impression that you don't have much to say to me, and that perhaps the reason for that is that you don't ..."

'"... have much to report," I said, completing her sentence.

'"So to speak," she conceded.

'I confessed.

'"No, I suppose I don't have many friends. When I think about it anyway. Though, really, I never did."

'She looked at me for a moment.

'"Well that's just terrible. My gosh. Poor you. That's just terrible. To be alone all this time in London. Do you not have *any* friends?"

'The sympathy concealed the puerile pleasure in the question that, at the time of our first meeting, she would never have thought to conceal.

'"No, not really. I don't know anyone in London."

'"Not from school or university?" she asked.

'I shook my head.

'"Well that's just terrible," she repeated. "Why did you come to London, if you don't know anybody?" she asked.

'"For my job. I wanted to do this job," I replied.

'"And have you not made any friends through your job?" she asked.

'"I wouldn't say 'friends'. I've got to know some people."

'By this time, she seemed to be looking down on me from a great height, and trotting through her questions, so that she might soon be free of my company.

"'What do you do?" I asked.

"'I'm a writer," she replied quickly. "I write for … a magazine. And I am about to publish a novel."

"'Congratulations, that's quite an achievement," I said. "What's it about?"

"'It's broadly political in theme – though I suppose you could say moral and political. It's based around a sort of unholy trinity of characters: a priest, his daughter, and a young political agitator. The plot turns a chiastic structure; a young girl who is born into a traditional family and a position of privilege, whose worldview is challenged by the current of change, by a more progressive perspective … all of which is symbolised by the political agitator. As a young woman, in a sense she symbolises Eros, torn between different objects of desire, and I suppose the tension turns on where the *true* object of desire lies. Naturally, as someone educated and conditioned by the world of privilege and tradition she, at first, sees nothing desirable about the political agitator and his *weltanschauung*. But – and hence the chiastic structure – as the novel progresses, its moral universe inverts."

"'What happens to the priest?" I asked.

"'He is exposed as a hypocrite," she replied curtly.

"'Well, I hope it will be a great success, and I will look out for it in the shops. Perhaps I could get a signed copy?"

"Of course," she laughed, "but look, never mind about my book. There are more important things, aren't there? I have to say that I find it truly extraordinary that I am the first person who has offered to do this – if am, then, really, I don't know what the world is coming to – but perhaps you would like me to introduce you to some people? I have a number of friends and, let me think, I believe we are meeting at a friend's house this coming weekend for a party. If you like, you are more than welcome to come along. They are all very friendly and will, I am sure, be very glad to meet you."

'"That's very kind of you ..." for some reason I remember I thought for a long while before I continued, "... yes, I would be ... I think I would like that."

'"There is just one thing. I may be doing you an injustice since the last time we met we were a lot younger and, well, as you might expect, much more *immature*, but I seem to remember that you were very quiet. You may very well have changed ... I don't know ... but my friends will try to make conversation with you and they will – how shall I put it? – they will expect you to pay them back in kind. Most of them are quite ebullient characters. Not that I am suggesting you are uninteresting or in any way ... but it is just something to bear in mind. You should also be aware that I won't tolerate prudishness. Some of my friends are very liberal-minded. Particularly about their sexuality. We do not tread on eggshells around the subject of fornic ... when it comes to *fucking*" ... she emphasised this word in a way that sounded odd and incongruous to me.

'"Of course," I said.

'She looked at me in a way that could not conceal her suspicion that this message had not properly penetrated my skull.

"'Anyway, it's just something to bear in mind. It's just, I suppose, a little odd that you have been in London all this time and not ... I mean this is *London*. I find it hard to imagine what life must be like without a group of friends. I'm sorry to labour the point – you may remember that I like to speak my mind. But don't you think that ... I mean surely without society there is just insanity, isn't there?"

'She eyed me suspiciously when she asked this question.

"'Surely some sort of society is part of our evolutionary success as a species?" she continued.

"'Perhaps," I said, "but by that logic the word 'misanthrope' or even just 'loner' would have no meaning. But it clearly does. And given that's the case, maybe the question is 'why?'"

'She withdrew into temporary silence.

"'I didn't mean to offend you," she said eventually. "Honestly, I didn't. This may sound like a trivial point – you know, the petty-minded observation of someone concerned *only* with social niceties. But it isn't. An awful lot ... well, in my view anyway, an awful lot hangs on conversation, on articulating, and learning to articulate."

"'Mmm," I said, not really sure what to say."

III

David approaches the large banks of sand that overwhelm the road just before the lighthouse. He stops, or hesitates. The part of him that does not want to meet the man just yet wants to put a few more minutes in the way of his next lesson. He dismounts his bicycle and wheels it forward, peering around the mountain of sand to see if the man is in sight. Even from a distance, he can see that the main entrance to the lighthouse remains padlocked. This is odd. Assuming that the man is inside the lighthouse, how does he manage to lock the padlock on the outside? It seems obvious that the man must be *outside* the lighthouse.

Through the corner of his eye he can see the shipwreck. He turns his head to look at it directly, and thinks about prolonging a meeting with the man by examining it further. It doesn't look quite as sodden as it did before, but it stands out in the same way, and nothing else about it has changed. He begins to wonder what must have happened to the rest of the ship. Is there a whole ship buried underneath the sand or jutting out into the shallow waters off the peninsula? Or is the ship the remnant of an accident that occurred at sea, or a collision that occurred further up the coast and which has bounced off the coastline's ragged promontories, finally lodging in the sticky sand at the mouth of the river? David thinks that the ship must be old because it has the shapelessness of old age.

"Hey there!" a voice calls out from above.

David looks upwards sharply. He can just see the tip of the man's head peering out of the topmost window, or porthole, of the lighthouse.

"Yes, it's me," says the man. "I'm up here."

David gives him a cheery wave.

"I was hoping you would return. I have been thinking about our last meeting. Perhaps I can avail you of my thoughts!"

The man walks out of the lighthouse's front door before David knows it and before he has time to think how he managed to unlock the padlock from the inside (was it really locked?). He strolls up to David in a way that displays firmness of character and purpose. He extends his arms in greeting. David shakes the hand. The man's grip is just as firm.

"Very good to see you again, David. It was a real pleasure to meet you last time. As you might imagine, I don't get to meet many people out here. And of course, I have been thinking about everything that was — and in some cases wasn't — said the last time we met. And I have more to tell you. I can see by the look in your eyes that this news stirs in you a spring of excitement and relish! Well, be that as it may. I can also see that you are clearly very interested in the shipwreck. That, if I remember rightly, was where I found you the last time we chanced upon each other (or I chanced upon you). I think I can see why you might be interested in the shipwreck. People often are. I see them from the top of my lighthouse, circling it, climbing on top of it, sticking their beaks into its smited jaws."

"The last time I came here, you said that the story you were telling me — about the bossy girl — took place between the lighthouse and the shipwreck. But it didn't. It took place a long time ago and in a different place."

"So, you *were* paying attention. Perhaps you are one of those pupils who very studiously and quietly assimilate all the information and then unleash on their unfortunate tutor a deluge of questions. So, what did you conclude from that? Did you think it was just an inconsistency? That I hadn't got my facts straight?"

"No, I just wondered what you meant?"

"I am sure it must have a part to play. If, as you said, I said it was significant, then *obviously*, it must be significant. Don't you think?"

"Yes, I suppose so," says David, a little nonplussed.

David has surprised himself. This question had occurred to him in the last few days, and he had decided that he would pluck up the courage to ask it at some point during in his next meeting. But he had not thought he would manage to ask it quite so soon, in such a direct way, or that it would return anything of any value. Now that the answer to the question has vindicated his decision to ask it, he feels suddenly engaged in the man's story — there is, he thinks, something faint and for the moment indecipherable that he can get out of this story. He decides that, from now on, he will concentrate hard, that he will watch the man intently with his eyebrows crouched over his eyes, waiting to leap out at an obvious point to query.

"Do you like English muffins?" asks the man.

David is not expecting this question, and immediately his brain begins to make associations with muffins. He calls on all his previous experience of muffins, and tries, in a split second, to spot connections with the story, with lighthouses, shipwrecks, with attractive but redoubtable girls (even a connection with a blubbering bottom might be something).

But he soon hits the wall of his knowledge and experience in this area. He is not sure he really knows the difference between an English muffin and a muffin of any other national provenance. And, if it comes to that, he is not sure he has actually ever eaten a muffin. He knows he has eaten a crumpet before now, and thinks that muffins belong to the same family of afternoon-tea snacks, but he is not sure exactly what form they take. He is confident that, like scones, they would go well with jam.

"Yes," he says with his confidence not clearly visible.

"Would you like to join me for one?"

"For a muffin?"

"Yes, for a muffin."

"Okay," says David, who is still wondering if there is a subtext to this question, or if the man is just being generous with his muffins.

"It is a beautiful day," says the man, observing the clear blue sky and the brilliant sun, "could we eat outside, do you think? On the beach."

David trundles his bicycle down the beach, and plunges into the sand between the lighthouse and the shipwreck adjacent to a row of old wooden groynes which disappears into the sea. His mind switches between the significance of muffins – which he is starting to suspect don't have any significance – and a creeping feeling that a picnic on the beach is not a million miles away from a bag of liquorice in a municipal park.

Should he make like the wind and return to the protection of his family, playing it safe with his publicly funded education? Or is it too late for that? If he runs now, will the man come hounding after him, lumbering down the broken track, blundering past the buttocks, to root out his prey? David envisages knocks on his window in the middle of the night, and the face of the man, pressing up against the glass as though the moon itself were trying to break into his bedroom. If he neglects the man now, he thinks that the man might stalk him for the rest of his life, appearing at occasional times (through his school window, as he is playing football with his friends, on the campus when he goes to university, in the car park on the premises of his first job) as the man chooses the right moment to strike. A new flood of panic spreads throughout his body. What has he let himself in for? It would have been much more sensible to confine his education to books, numbers, and a crippling fear of his peers.

"They are still warm," says the man, obviously excited by the comestibles he is carrying in a cloth.

If this spread is designed to entice David, the underlying malevolence is well concealed; the man seems to be enjoying himself too much, to the point where David's presence has become merely an excuse to tuck in.

The man sits down next to David and opens the cloth in which he has wrapped the bread. Steam evaporates into the air as David picks out the latest object of his curiosity.

"The cultivation of the mind and the cultivation of the body are one and the same. Brain food is essential to any education. In my view, government policy makers should seriously consider a fund to encourage the consumption of quality food: delectable foods for delectable thoughts."

David weighs the muffin between the palms of his hands.

"I don't understand," he says suddenly, feeling emboldened.

"Would you like something with it? I usually eat them as they are – I have flavoured them with cheddar and black pepper."

"I don't mean that. I mean I don't understand it all. All the things you said last time, about the lighthouse and about the girl. It doesn't ... I can't understand how ... and I looked in a book ... in an encyclopaedia ... and I spoke to someone else ... everything says that lighthouses are meant to warn ships."

"Oh, I see," says the man who is grinding hard on his muffin. "I thought you were talking about ... yes, well you would think so, I agree. Certainly that's how it *seems*."

"But these were ... it was an *encyclopaedia*."

"Oh, I don't doubt that what you are saying appears in the encyclopaedia, or that it is common knowledge. If you were to place someone who had never seen a lighthouse before in front of a lighthouse, they could probably work out the purpose you are attributing to them. It's the most intuitive explanation. But it's only how it seems. *Not* how it is. Is that a difference that you understand?"

"I'm not sure."

The man looks out to sea and points at something.

"You see that freight liner on the horizon?"

David squints.

"Yes."

"Well, from here it looks like a relatively long way away, doesn't it? But if I were to fetch my binoculars and we were to look at it through them, the ship would *seem* much closer. In that instance, the binoculars create the illusion that is recognised by our intuition, which sees things as they are. But suppose that intuition is not always the template for reality. If you ever look at yourself in a reflection, the image is distorted, and anything that appears under the water is also distorted. So, things as they appear aren't always altogether reliable. And that's the case with the lighthouse. It appears as a building for warning ships and the common understanding sees them in this way too. But its origins are quite different. So, to get back to these origins, it will be necessary to approach things as they appear with a touch – just a touch – of scepticism, a kind of boldness in the face of everything taken for granted."

David takes a bite out of his muffin, and is temporarily distracted by how good it tastes. He doesn't say anything.

"To see the difference between the way the ship appears to the naked eye and the way it appears through the binoculars is easy. But the alternative education I am offering you is different. It requires you to *imagine*. It requires you to imagine that, in some sense, intuition is not unlike the distorting influence of the binoculars or the trickery in the ripples of a running stream. This education is not like running up against a brick wall and asking you to account for every single brick. It says that every brick wall you encounter is built on insecure foundations. To my way of thinking that makes education a little less frightening, and a little more consoling for those who are the muffins of the academic world rather than the *crème de la crème*."

David is pleasantly surprised by the muffin and prefers to keep eating; though he is paying attention to the man. It seems like a good moment to eat and listen.

"So, in many ways the history of the lighthouse is caught between a history of how things seem and how things are, and its history explores whether there is ever any reconciliation between the two. Which brings me back to my story about Isobel. You see, when I first met her, when we were both teenagers, the way I thought things were, turned out to be only the way they seemed. But to explain that, I need to jump ahead.

'When I was a young man, I got a job as a junior librarian at the Courtauld Institute."

IV

"The party was in South West London in a large four-storeyed house that had once been Victorian slums. None of the floors were especially big. There were two, maybe three, rooms on each floor. All quite poky. But there were so many people that they had dispersed equally among the floors. I spent the first half hour wandering between the floors, trying to find the only person I knew. Eventually I found her in the roof garden talking to a foreign journalist who spoke poor English. He was Italian, I think, and he was congratulating her on her book.

'She introduced me.

'"This is a friend," she said. "I think I mentioned that I had invited a friend."

'"A friend or a *boy*friend?" the journalist asked, nearly singing his question.

'"Oh ... no, it's nothing like that," she laughed. "Sonny and I knew each other as children, and we ran into each other earlier in the week. He is ... he is relatively new to London, so I thought I should ... Sonny works as a librarian at the Courtauld Institute."

'The Italian looked me up and down with a sort of histrionic pride, like a cartoon gladiator.

'She introduced me to other people. Let me see. There was a whole host of colourful characters. A few people in the theatre. Her publisher was there. Lawyers, musicians, artists (aspiring and established), and a whole army of young journalists, draining the house of alcohol, like a field of crop sucking up nutrients.

'At what point it happened, I don't know, as I had by that time had quite a bit to drink myself. But at some point in one of those many rooms on one of those four floors, someone said something that caught the attention of everyone in the room. It must have been a living room of some kind because I was sitting on the floor leaning against the end of a sofa, as girls in miniskirts stretched their long legs out on the linoleum.

'"Change," said the voice, "that's what we are experiencing – change. We are overseeing the gradual disintegration of an established order: the class system, the church, the army (God, the fucking army!)" – there were laughs – "we might even burn down the House of fucking Lords!"

'There were more laughs.

'"You could characterise it in all kinds of ways: changes for women, for people from different ethnic groups, for homosexuals. It's all change. A group of people have come along and they have looked at the status quo and seen that the status quo is a wake-up call. And they have pushed back the horizon of reality to the point where the status quo looks absurd."

'Except the man – if it was a man – didn't say this. I just made this up. It's been such a long time, and I was drunk, so I don't really know what they said. But this is the sort of thing they would have said or might have said. Something to do with change and addressing the injustices of society, from the landed gentry to grammar schools, from sexual mores to grammar.

'"It is an act of unveiling; peeling back the lace curtains to look at the truth," said the voice.

'Though again, he wouldn't have said that. Or if he did say anything vaguely like that, he would not have said it in those terms. I have made it sound like a piece of political rhetoric, and no-one is ever as coherent as a piece of political rhetoric. No, I am exaggerating. You must excuse the hyperbole."

"The what?"

"Hyp ... the exaggeration. So, keeping that in mind, let's assume the voice continued. And let's assume that he said something like this:

"'Ostensibly we are the children of an earlier generation, whose wisdom we are meant to inherit. But in the history of progress, I think that we are the parents and they are children. I have a degree from a good university, yes? Does that mean that I should sign on at a gentleman's club and start singing songs like 'When the Partridge Pots his Luck' or 'Burp like Horatio!' Or a career in politics – I take a formal first in Greats and in-between a thousand chicken dinners I realise that – oddly enough – Orpheus and Eurydice are *not* relevant to the complex socio-economic problems of the day!

"'Or the church – I mean literally where do you stop? Here is a society that in the best traditions of its 'High Anglican' heritage, gives public space to a doddering old fool with a voice like English oak to impart platitudes of wisdom based on a few books he read at theological college, and whose real interest is potted plants, steam engines and the head of the girl guides. Even the word Anglican lacks conviction – all it means is a political fudge between the smells and bells of the Catholic tradition, and a theology that is, in theory at least, informed.

"'Any form of change hinges on an 'if only'. If only the education system could grant to a greater number of people the privileges that many of us have enjoyed, then would not more people see that these so-called bulwarks of our society and culture are a joke!

'"Our obscurantist rites and superstitions look like the idiotic ramblings of a child. And that analogy is very real. A hundred years from now, maybe even twenty or thirty years from now when, if Mr Wilson is to be believed, the white heat of the technological revolution will have transformed our judgements, the status quo probably will seem as laughable as the beliefs of a child. Well it is, isn't it? Is that right? If you think back ... the things you were taught as children ... the things you believed ... go on — what did you believe? I challenge you!"

'I repeat that the voice — if it was just one voice — did not say these exact words. I have skipped over things, misremembered certain other things, and made the words that were actually spoken more articulate than they were.

'There followed several anecdotes from the childhoods of individuals at the party: someone reprimanded for carrying a piece of paper too 'noisily'; another who became so frightened of hell that they prayed seven or eight times a day.

'And it was at this stage that Isobel raised her voice, and, in an effort to include me, I suppose, told the world about my theory.

'"When I knew Sonny," she said, "... we were only children ... we had this silly idea that everything was circular. I don't suppose it was anything we had inculcated into us, but all the same. Did you just make it up, Sonny?"

'I nodded.

'"We thought that because the world was round, everything was round – so any event would come around again. And we would imagine what it would be like if we were eternally repeating ourselves."

'She smiled at me.

'"Well some of our national institutions are no less ridiculous," said the voice.

'So this is how it happened. I don't suppose it was that sudden. I mean, I don't suppose that through my alcoholic haze I suddenly thought "All that stuff I thought as a child was actually a load of rubbish". No, no. Not at all. My thoughts had changed. Naturally they had changed. I had been educated. I had been to *university*. In the course of growing up, I suppose I had unconsciously shelved the ideas that I had dreamed up during the first summer that I met Isobel. But I had never actually stopped to think – or confess, you might say – that these ideas were clearly silly, *childish* even. And only by having the ideas ridiculed publicly in this way did I realise that the way things *seemed* as a child was clearly not the way they *were*. Not if the company I was keeping was anything to go by.

'I didn't really know why at the time, because it was not as though I actually believed in my theory, but the mention of it and its association with my childhood made me feel subdued. I did not feel strongly one way or the other about the views of the voice. But his views made me feel grown up – and adulthood, whether or not I agreed with what was said, had given me a perspective from which I could see my ideas as a child for what they were. But here's the paradox – the uncorrected interests and giddy expression of strange ideas I had when I was young came with a kind of confidence, a chirruping, trilling train of expression, even if it was barely sensible. On the other hand, now that I could see these ideas soberly and sensibly, I had exploded that confidence. How was it possible that I was so much happier carried along by the whimsical meanderings of my childhood mind than by the clear and distinct perspective of knowledge and education? It should have been the other way around.

'And when I thought briefly about the time I had spent with Isobel when we were teenagers, even in my henpecked state, it seemed trouble-free and unsullied out of all proportion to the so-called reality from which I was now looking back on it with an ironic glint. This unasked-for act of looking back, had me by the throat and was preparing to squeeze."

V

"How many weeks is it now? Till you go back to school?"

"One."

David has been counting the days since the last week in July. He has been chalking up a mental tally. The last week in August, which amounts to the last gasp of summer, adds to the sense of impending misery. The evenings are beginning to draw in and the world around him is positioning itself for a change, hungover on too much sun. The village and even more popular stretches of the coastline have reverted to an out-of-season quietness. There are fewer people, fewer cars, fewer geriatric holidaymakers carrying their tartan blankets down to the sea; and all the seasonal entrepreneurs have sniffed the economic wind and followed the scent of another viable market.

"One. That's not a very long time."

"No."

"And are you looking forward to it? I mean are you excited about your new school."

David doesn't say anything.

"Because I mean it must present opportunities. Do you think you might encounter individuals who inspire you to learn, who instil in you a love of knowledge for its own sake? You might make friends and build the foundations of a gregarious personality and social networking skills that leave you made for life. You might discover a passion for sports, for football, rugby, cricket. Or maybe you'll take to the theatre. There must be many opportunities."

David looks at the ground sadly.

"I went to buy a blazer and a tie. And a badge. And a sweatshirt for PE."

Buying these objects had not been like any other purchase. Attached to them was the stigma of everything they foreshadowed. Once his mum had stitched the badge onto his blazer, David had tried on the full uniform, parading in front of a mirror in the bathroom. He had felt conflicted about it; the superficial pleasure of a new set of clothes was tarnished when he thought about their purpose.

"You don't sound too excited about it."

"No," David admitted.

"Why is that?"

The man interrogates David for a moment, searching through the edges of his rotund visage.

"You can be honest with me. We have established that, I think. I want you to be honest with me."

David brushes the crumbs of his muffin off his T-shirt and into the sand. A light breeze skirts off the surface of the water and ruffles his hair. He looks out to sea.

"The closer I get to going to school, I get this *feeling*."

"What feeling?"

"I don't know. Like I'm hollow on the inside. And I keep getting more hollow. I don't know what it is."

"I do."

David looks at the man, hoping for an explanation, but for once the man won't offer his thoughts and his eyes cover the stretch of water now neglected by David.

"Sometimes things aren't as bad as you think they are going to be," says the man, still looking out to sea. "Sometimes the worst part is all the anticipation, and it's not so bad when it actually comes to doing it. You may find that after your first week or month, you love your new school. It does happen like that sometimes.

But then at other times it doesn't. At other times, you spend weeks and weeks fretting and worrying over something, lying in bed tormented by the shadows cast on the ceiling by the light of the morning. And then it so happens that everything you were worrying about comes to pass, and is in fact even worse than the morbid fantasies of your imagination. That's my experience anyway."

David dares to ask a question that rises up inside him, riding on a wave of hope.

"What about me? How do you think I will find it?"

"I wouldn't altogether distrust that hollow feeling inside you. But perhaps you might put it to good work in the time that remains. You should use it to galvanise a will to understand the purpose of this lesson. Don't let it eat you up. Because it *will* try to."

David thinks about the man's instruction through a grimace. And with this prompt he can, for the first time, feel the different threads of his alternative 'education' beginning to dovetail: his journey to the end of the peninsula, the lighthouse, and its peculiar history.

Until now, all these elements have seemed disparate and incompatible, but he can begin to see that there might be points of connection. He furrows his brow, thinks hard and pushes his Wellington boots into the sand.

"I am trying to understand the ... Isobel. The girl you knew."

"Go on."

"The first time you met her you talked a lot about your ideas. About circles and stuff."

"And?"
"The lighthouse is round."
"Yes?"
"Is that why?"
"Yes."
"So, the lighthouse ... is about that idea?"
"Yes."
"So, you told me about the girl to tell me about the idea?"
"I told you about Isobel to explain how I started thinking about the idea."
"Why couldn't you just explain the idea?"
"Because there is more to a lighthouse than its roundness. In any case, as I explained to you last time, there's more than one way to explain the lighthouse; I have told the story because that is the fullest and most accessible route."
"And now you're going to tell me more about the girl?"
"Yes."
"So, the girl has something more to do with the lighthouse?"
"Yes."
David chews on the cud of his intellectual energy, trying to tease out further conclusions.
"I can see you are trying to piece it all together. You have to be careful – the need to complete the picture can find solutions where they don't exist."
"It's a lot to think about. Like a riddle."
"Yes."

"I still don't really see how the girl and the lighthouse fit together. I don't see the exact connection between your ideas about circles and the lighthouse. And I don't know what you mean about the way things seem being different from real things. How does that fit into it?"

"You are getting impatient. Now the mist is starting to clear, you want to charge through it."

"And the shipwreck. What about the shipwreck?"

David begins drawing a line in the sand with his finger. He doesn't want to let go of the subject yet. So far this lesson has been a triumph. For once – for the first time – he has asked questions and they have returned answers that he was expecting. For once his understanding of things chimes with the way they are. Is this just the start? After a slow beginning, will he understand more and more, so that by the time he is middle-aged he will be picking holes in string theory? Or has he just collided by chance with the truth, only to return the next day to his default state of blind faith in his intellectual convictions? The uncertainty makes him want to seize the moment, to cling on while it is still working.

"What happened in-between?" he asks.

"I'm sorry?"

"What happened in-between the first time you met the girl when you were younger and the second time you met her, when you were in London?"

"Oh, not much really. It doesn't really matter. It doesn't have a bearing on the story."

"Didn't you think about her or anything?"

"I don't know. It doesn't matter. How about if I say 'I can't remember'. Does that work for you?"

"Well what about her? What did she do?"

"Again, it doesn't really matter. She went to Cambridge to study English literature. Who knows! She was packed off to Cheltenham Ladies College. She took up lacrosse with fervour. That sort of thing. You make it up, if you like."

"Do *you* know what happened in-between?"

"Only in so much as I lived through it. But for the purposes of the story, I have no idea. It really doesn't matter. Let it go."

"I don't understand *that* at all."

"Again, all in good time. Don't get carried away. Part of these conclusions that you are making is about letting the story tell itself. These things have a logic all of their own."

Even so, David cannot relinquish his hold on the story and its meaning. The connection between the man's childhood theory about circles and the circular shape of the lighthouse is grating against him. It is forcing his mind into its own dizzying vortex.

"What about the bits of the story you have already told me? How did you get from an idea about circles to a building? And why?"

"Yes, it's interesting. I mean, at the end of the day, the lighthouse is just bricks and mortar. Nothing more than that. You could disassemble it and rearrange it to look like a more conventional building or leave it lying as a pile of rubble. It's for what those bricks and mortar have been used that's important.

Their shape and architecture reflect an idea; and, in that sense, they are a tangible reminder, a placeholder for the memory of that idea."

"But why not just explain the idea; you wouldn't need the lighthouse at all?"

The moon refracts the light of a smile at David.

"I need the lighthouse for the same reason that you need it; for the same reason that you are sitting here; for the same reason you are exploring an alternative approach to your education. But you are right; in many ways it is inadequate. I sometimes like to sit and think about its shortcomings. Bricks, glass, wood – all dull materials, and combined they amount to something clumsy and crude. It follows the same restricted form of communication between motorists – a flash of the headlamp might mean any number of completely different things in the mind of different drivers, but that meaning is concealed by the blunt edges of the chassis. It's the same with the lighthouse; it is possible to imagine many different stories and explanations that might lie behind the building.

'So, you are right; it would be possible to communicate the idea in a more analytically precise way. But my feeling is that, for all its crudity, ambiguity and imprecision, the lighthouse is more effective because it has more impact. To explain the idea I would have to travel around widely or write it down in the hope that people would read what I have written. A building is a simple material construct, but it is more visually striking, and in my estimation more likely to strike a chord. Not everyone is capable of grasping an idea, but everyone can at least sense the idea through a particularly curious object. So, what it loses in meaning, it gains in impact.

'And in any case, as you will see, the nature of the idea itself leaves open the possibility for many different forms of communication (or simply many different forms) because to some extent it challenges the categorical legitimacy of all forms of communication. And if it is the case that no single form of communication – including the most analytically precise – does real justice to the idea, then maybe there is more to be gained through a form of communication, however crude, that speaks in an idiom to which more people can relate. Analysis, by this logic, would be a luxury but to an extent an illusion.

'So, as you might be able to see, on this peninsula, our educational goalposts are suited to the nature of the student as the ultimate nature of the object of study recedes behind a veil of mystery. The curriculum here is not as rigid as the government's.

'But in London I was being educated into the view that knowledge and education can overcome that veil of mystery, which, in a sense, means that the student is irrelevant, and must simply adapt to the reality described by his or her educators. The distinction between reality and appearance was so clear that you could create a whole system of comprehensive education at the drop of a hat.

'As you can see, there is more mileage yet in my story about Isobel. So I will continue. Our next meeting was at the party to which she had invited me.

'The party was in South West London in a large four-storeyed house that had once been Victorian slums."

VI

"One evening I was in *The Bullfinch*. You remember I told you that the owner of my flat worked for the metropolitan police force. He said he did a 'spot of administrative work' for them. Well anyway, one evening, not too long after the party, I had arranged to meet Isobel for an evening bite to eat. I had barely sat down when my neighbour hailed me from across the room and invited himself to a chair at my table. We ended up eating together. It was one of the first times that I had really talked to him.

'He did most of the talking. He would ask me questions and even allow me to answer them, but he would cut me short at a few sentences, and treat the whole exercise as an opportunity for him to talk at length about some aspect of his life. A simple question like "What brought you to London?" was really just a polite justification for his own answer to the question.

'"So, what brought you to London?" he asked me.

'The job, I explained.

'"Can't say that I have ever been more than a stone's throw away from the dirty old town. Of course, I hail from Berkshire. That's how my early life went: Berks, Caius Cambridge, London. I suppose, I should have been called to the bar, but I never felt altogether chummy with the theatre of logical pedantry. It's so easy to drift into the metropolitan police force. Perhaps, you might say, only for the discharge of certain civic duties! But for someone like me ... no, I suppose in truth I was always teetering on the edge of a different set of ambitions. Of course, I grew up in a village. Yes ... did you know that I once ate from the same tray that had served up afternoon tea to the 3rd Marquess of Salisbury? The tray was held in veneration, housed in its own sacred reliquary behind the oak diadarn. It was brought out only on special occasions – the Royal Birthday, the 1918 armistice, a sighting of the Sir Nigel Gresley ... that sort of thing. I can't recall what occasioned my eating from it. The family to whom it belonged were ... I think they felt the insecurity and pretensions of the parvenu. Something like that. Good heavens, is that a terribly judgemental things to say?"

'"No ... well, I don't know."

'"I have to rely upon people to correct me, you see. Not that I have many friends to whom I can easily turn. I hold dinner parties from time to time; but I'm not exactly a socialite. That, I find, is one of the many things that friends – true friends – are for. Correction. Or even just chivvying you along in the right direction, so to speak. But London, yes of course ... I mean of course it's a charming place, and only natural that ... well, it seemed that's what others did. Cambridge to London. It seemed that was the natural route to follow. I have to say, though, that for all my love of the dirty old town, its saffron evening mists, there is a part of me that thinks back … is that just sad, sentimental nostalgia, do you think?"

'Before I had the opportunity to answer the question (if he even wanted me to answer the it), Isobel arrived. She clearly seemed a little surprised to find me with my landlord.

'"Well now, I must be standing – or rather sitting – in the way. And sitting rather clumsily and greedily, I should have thought," my landlord said, standing up and dabbing his mouth with his napkin. "I take it you two are together romantically, or after some such fashion? Is that the case?"

'He was looking between me and Isobel for an explanation.

'"No, Sonny and I are only friends. Old friends, in fact. Please sit down. I had no idea that Sonny had arranged to meet you as well. Please do sit down. There's no need for …"

'My landlord sat down.

'"I'm afraid this was no *rendez vous*. Just a chance meeting," he explained. "We just had the good fortune – or perhaps we can get by without the epithet – to meet each other here with the same … how shall I put it? … gastronomic mission. But I know when an old office boy stands in the way of young blood. The political instincts of the bureaucrat are not that unrefined."

'Isobel sat down.

'"No, please. I am not being falsely polite. I would be happy to meet you."

'She fired a peculiar look at me.

'"Well if you insist I shall of course be delighted to join you. The food here is very much like the furniture – somewhat durable. But the ambience is cosmopolitan. I know it is unlikely, but I like to think that it is the sort of place that Whistler and his chums might have patronised.

'My landlord took an artificial pause.

'"So, I don't believe we have been properly introduced," he said, looking reproachfully at me.

'I apologised and introduced Isobel.

'"You are a novelist," he continued. "Well, that is something. That is really quite an achievement. Literature – true literature – is of course horribly underrated. I don't doubt that many people read, though they do say it's on the way out, don't they? The television, they say, is pulling off a cultural coup. But often things that people read ... the quality of literature. Potboilers. That's what they are. That's the trend. I could be wrong, but I have the impression that you write more erudite fiction."

'Isobel flicked her hair back.

'"I suppose you could say that it's thematic," she replied.

'My landlord nodded his head.

'"Yes, thematic; because many of these books don't have themes, do they? They're all tennis coaches and jodhpurs and a cat's cradle of deceit and avarice in an estuary setting. Or so I envisage.

"Your *friend* and I were just talking about the past. And it's interesting because, you see, where I grew up there was a voluntary association of ladies who took over the parish hall once a month to partake of tea, pastries and an improving diet of literature. They called themselves *The Elevenses and Literature Society*.

"I believe it was often held to good account by the young gentlemen-cum-rogues of the village that this literary ensemble was really an excuse to practise a more covert interest. From the overexcited, and at times positively vile, imagination of young men, I am sure you can extract some flavour of these rumours. The more simple – you might say safe – imaginings envisaged these ladies parading around the village all in their under-things to "compare the seasonal fashions". Others were ... more darkly perverse. But if you were ever to meet any of these ladies you would soon realise how altogether uncharacteristic such fantasies were.

"On one occasion a group of these young boys placed a wooden bench underneath the elongated window of the parish hall. From there, they peered in at the hermetic rituals enacted on the inside. It so happened that the day they chose coincided with a week in which the ladies had been reading a now out-of-print work about gentlewomen corrupted by rogue highwaymen. As the young scallywags were peering into the village hall, the ladies happened to be enacting a scene of heightened drama from the book; to convey a measure of verisimilitude, two of the ladies had placed stockings over their heads, and were waving parasols rather menacingly at their partners. This so exceeded even the most grotesque expectation of the young miscreants that one of them fell off the bench and tumbled to the ground with a clatter. This alerted the ladies to their presence, and there a followed a pursuit: several young men hounded by middle-aged women wearing stockings on their heads and brandishing works of nineteenth century romantic literature as their chosen weapon of the war. For exegetical purposes, I believe one of the ladies had brought with her a particularly ponderous volume of Feuerbach.

'Oh you must excuse me," continued my landlord. "I do go on … sometimes I am told in quite a dithyrambic way … so I apologise if I offend you."

'Isobel had listened attentively throughout the story but without imparting any warmth; her smiles saddled an unchecked instinct to laugh and politeness; she couldn't seem to chart the course of her opinion in this case.

'"Not at all; it's interesting to hear your story," she replied. "It does seem to me – and I am aware that I am perhaps prejudging you – that you are representative … or, if not representative exactly, then an example of an older set of values, and a culture that perhaps belongs more to the first half of the twentieth century than the second."

'My landlord laughed.

'"Well, heavens, that's bold!" he said.

'"Oh, I didn't mean to be rude," Isobel said hurriedly.

'My landlord was still smiling.

'"No, not rude exactly. Though 'he belongs more to the first half of the twentieth century than the second' sounds a little like a sardonic epitaph of which one might almost feel proud."

'Isobel continued.

'"But it is interesting don't you think? How things change, I mean?"

'My landlord raised his eyebrows.

'"Interesting in what way?" he asked.

'Isobel looked, if possible, even more intense.

'"I mean you could almost be a character in a book around which a particular point of tension revolves, a sort of fulcrum for the overall dynamic of the story. You, it seems to me, belong to a very particular world, and, historically, that particular world has exercised a privileged position in society."

'My landlord looked downcast.

'"I hope I'm not going to end up parodied by your pen," he said rolling his eyes.

'Isobel came back with a little too much aggression.

'"Is that really your worst fear?" she asked candidly.

'"No I suppose it isn't," he replied, "but my current estimation of this table and its three patrons is that one views me with the respect that human beings generally have for their landlords, and the other sees me as a foil in an as yet unwritten work of radical fiction. Either way the outlook is bleak."

'Isobel smiled.

'"I'll try to explain, but I'll tell it to you as a story. That's my preferred idiom."

'Isobel gave me a look of moment and meaning, which I was not able to interpret.

'My landlord leaned back in his chair.

'"Well, if that's your preferred idiom ..." he said.

'Isobel began.

'"Really, the story follows a chiastic structure. I won't go into all the details. It will be enough to set out ..."

"What's a chiastic structure?"

"Beats me. I'm just the narrator."

"Oh. Okay."

"As I was saying, or rather as Isobel was saying in my account of the events ...

'"It will be enough to set out a basic outline, which goes something like this: there is a young girl ..."

'My landlord interrupted her.

'"This is the heroine we are talking about?" he asked.

'"Perhaps," she conceded, "though something of an anti-heroine in some ways."

'My landlord nodded his head.

'"A subtle story of internal contradictions and ambiguities. Very good. Go on, go on."

'Isobel drew air.

'In some ways the story is quite straight-forward. The girl's outlook and assumptions about the world are conditioned by her social and economic background. Which is privileged. I suppose you might even say that she has a slightly deluded view of her own significance, and has even been brought up to think – by her education and peers – that she will occupy a position of some social standing in her society.

'But gradually, as she grows up, she encounters individuals who change her outlook. Naturally – since this is only a story – the complex nature of these changes are rolled into, or personified by, only a handful of situations and carefully selected scenarios. The main character is a young man with whom she falls in love. And it is through this attraction to the young man that she is encouraged to think about the world in a slightly different way; because he is from a less privileged background, and exemplifies the tensions that entail a society that derives it values from social class.

'When she first meets this young man, he is aggressive towards her, he is snide and sardonic, he verbally castigates her and everything that she represents; there is even – since this is a fiction – a frisson of sexual violence. Naturally enough this challenge to her background and social standing leaves her upset at first; but gradually, as she learns more about the man, as she comes to appreciate things from his point of view, and – more than anything else – the more she reads and educates herself about the world, she finds that she can empathise with him, and moreover she finds herself attracted to him and everything he represents: integrity, ideology, a cynical assault on the prevailing 'wisdom' of the day."

'Unthinkingly, I opened my mouth at this point.

'"This is the story of your book, isn't it?" I said.

'I immediately grasped that the look Isobel had given me earlier had been intended to guard against giving away this information, as though she had been saying "Watch this, and don't give anything away!"

'My landlord, perhaps because he could begin to see where this was leading, hid behind formality.

'"It sounds like an interesting and exciting work that I am sure will captivate audiences," he said.

'Isobel replied acerbically.

'"Well, I am no slave to the whims of my audience, so that is not necessarily the whole point," she said.

'My landlord leaned forward in his chair.

'"And, to press you further, how does this underline my place in the first half of our century?"

'Isobel's eyes narrowed.

'"Well I suppose the point is just how fragile the axioms that underpin a culture are. One is encouraged to see things from a certain perspective, without calling that into question. But it perhaps takes brave souls – braver than you or I – to do just that. The account of things that they offer can expose injustices and errors. Which is why I say that education, study, learning ... all of these things are so important."

'My landlord looked across the room.

'"So, I am an anachronism? Or else, soon will be? This is what you are saying, yes?"

'She softened.

'"I am not making a heavy-handed judgement. The main protagonist of my story is a victim of her culture. You might even say she was poorly educated. Knowledge has for a long time (since the fifth century BC at least) been construed as an illuminating force; it is only through the continued pursuit of knowledge that the light it sheds can do any good. And I am sorry if I sounded a little blunt just now, but when you consider the importance of education, it seems to me that one cannot afford to fritter away words simply to please one's audience and earn a quick buck, or even to spend time writing material admired only for its rhetorical colour. That signals only a loss of integrity and purpose."

'My landlord looked across the other side of the room.

'"So it is a didactic story and one from which I would do well to learn?" he asked.

'Isobel recoiled in a slightly wounded fashion.

'"I can't help but feel that you are intent only on trivialising what I am trying to say. But I am sure anything bold and different meets with a challenge."

'A moment of consideration followed, and then my landlord spoke.

'"I'm sorry," he said, and thought his way forward. "But you are right to say that I find it challenging."

'Isobel interrupted.

'"If this is just going to turn into a protracted insult, then perhaps I should just leave now?" she said.

'My landlord shook his head.

'"Good Lord, we are not trading body blows yet are we? Stick around, stick around! We have some way to go still."

'Isobel frowned, and my landlord persevered.

'"At the risk of stereotyping, I would characterise my thoughts like this: it is easy for a younger generation like yours to look back on another generation, or even a group of individuals from a different social class to look on another social class, and make judgements based on the 'knowledge' that generation or class takes for granted. But suppose there is a future generation that will look back on the 1960s and see them solely in terms of an aesthetic unique to that period, which by that time looks dated and even quaint. 'Free love', 'CND' and the 'countercultural movement' will become the chapters in a history book written by an academic trying to make good on their advance. If that's the case then any attempt to make a judgement will look obscure, even arcane, given enough time. In which case, far from illuminating, the 'knowledge' coveted by any one individual, any one generation, class or culture, amounts to a vain groping about in the dark."

'Isobel stood up to leave.

'"That sounds like landlord's logic to me: a simple excuse not to care. Goodbye, Sonny."

'And she left."

VII

David struggles to concentrate. The age-old battle between the mind and body has developed into a particularly intense conflict. His different preoccupations appear one on top of the other, like a cinematic palimpsest created by a directorial brain gone wrong. His image of Isobel, the girl in the man's story, appears grafted onto the body of the girl that runs the heritage centre; he imagines himself the first time he visited the lighthouse, walking around it repeatedly, mapping out the physical trajectory of the idea to which the man has referred, as though the building gains concrete form from a more abstract source of life. In each of the different characters the man has described, David sees vestiges of the man's character, and to the extent that he can picture the way any of them might look, they all resemble the voice that provides the narration, so that David is never able to see these characters independently of their immediate source of life; and flashes of light spread across the turbulent seas of these hard-connecting images from the lighthouse as he envisages it at night. Only the source of light is not artificial; it comes from a natural source that refracts off the face of the man as he patrols the watchtower.

"To come back to a point I made earlier, something had changed between the first and the second time I met Isobel. I mean obviously things had changed. We were older. We paid rent. We drank alcohol. All important differences, I am sure. But something else had changed. The way things were when we were younger had become only the way they seemed. And they had become only a matter of appearance because we could by that stage explain those appearances by reference to a fuller picture of reality verified by institutions of learning and a consensus of like-minded young people. It made me very uncomfortable."

"How had the man learned these explanations?" thinks David. Surely they are things that he picked up when he was much older than David is now. If that were the case, then it implies that David is rooted firmly in naivety, waiting for his illusion-smashing education to ride over the horizon. It somehow invalidates any effort he might make to follow the lead of his mentor before he can even start. Logically speaking, it puts him in an impossible situation because his age and lack of education create the conditions for his ignorance.

Does this mean that the first tentative steps he has made with the man in these two lessons have been futile? If so, what could the man possibly be thinking? Why hold out the prospect of an education only to demonstrate that it is a waste of time? Unless the man wants to share with David lessons that he would otherwise only learn at an older age? David reasons that either the former conclusion entails or else the man holds out some suspicion of the education that makes the natural ignorance of his age possible.

David's brain more or less whirs.

"Of course, it is one thing to think those things privately ... Have you travelled much, David? In other parts of the country or abroad?"

"No, not much. I have been to Cornwall, and the Lake District."

"But most of your time, you have spent here?"

"Yes, I suppose so."

"I am interested to know what you think – do you think that there are many people in this part of the world?"

"No, not many."

"No. Sometimes it almost feels like you could count them."

"Yes, perhaps."

"And do you ever speak to them?"

"Not very much."

"Not if you can help it, huh?"

David smiles.

"I grew up in a similar environment. Travelling carries with it a certain cachet. A well-travelled person is a well-cultured person, someone who has sought to experience and understand a way of living and thinking other than their own. It is a case of quite literally broadening your horizons, becoming more open-minded.

'I travelled a little after I left London; nothing very exotic. But I went here and there. And I have to say that, though it does give you a broader perspective, in the same way that reading a book gives you a broader perspective, it *can* become just another form of education; another way of, so to speak, highlighting the inadequacies of something else. And – as with growing up and looking back on my childhood – I can't help but think that I was at my happiest, my most untroubled and liberated, when I was a young man growing up in a remote part of the world, where the impositions of human intelligence were, at best, a fringe activity."

"What are you saying?" David asks, his curiosity becoming bolder.

"I don't know," replies the man a little plaintively. "What am I saying? Education is fundamental. You only have to listen to governments. I mean it *is* fundamental, isn't it? How can you make a correct judgement about something without first understanding the thing that you are judging? How can you critique a painting, or comment on the magnificence of a work of architecture if you have never seen it? But what if your understanding, or your vision, is limited in some way, so that you can only see part of the image at which you are looking? Surely that means that your ability to judge is also limited? And that means 'proof' of education, and the power of judgement can always be questioned. Do I sound like a cynic?"

David looks puzzled.

"I don't know."

David is lost in the lesson, in how any of this relates to the lighthouse, or how it fits into the story about Isobel that the man had been telling. Is the man a disillusioned secondary school teacher, he wonders? Is he someone who committed some offence, took to drinking heavily, and withdrew to the lighthouse? Whether he is or he isn't, David feels sure that there is a simpler way to convey the lesson that the man wants to communicate. And he returns again to the feeling of frustration that all of these lessons are emphatically something which adults should take on board, and which are clearly not suitable for young boys who still have difficulty remembering the best way to calculate long division.

"What am I saying? I am saying that the idea of adulthood is a disappointment – worse than that, it is a myth, and it is a myth propagated by those who have the most at stake in its survival: adults. It is a story told by adults, for adults, a story told with self-serving logic for 'professionals' and people who talk in 'isms'. I am saying that the idea of adulthood is one big con, and you shouldn't believe it. Their authority is metaphysically spurious, and yet they wield it with gladiatorial aggression and confidence. Don't believe adults – they are stupid, wrong-headed, arrogant, bullying, ambitious, manipulative, cowardly and cretinous.

'I am saying that growing up to find that knowledge gives you the authority to pass judgement on something as casually as you would climb out of bed, left me feeling gloomy and unhappy. And this is why I say that you should live in fear of what is about to happen to you; you are right to be frightened. You are about to be jounced and jostled between one crazy, hare-brained attempt to make sense of things and another, some of which you will understand, some of which you won't; some of which you will remember, some of which you will forget."

David feels reassured by this assault on the world of adults. He has for some time (and aside from his general foreboding) felt wary of adulthood. He has assumed, until now, that this is just a feature of his age, and that everything will become clear in time: why, for example, adults cavort in a Babylonian rampage of destruction down the streets of towns on a Friday night; why they covet expensive cars designed by Germans; why they aspire to feelings of superiority; why they invented fish fingers. These are all great questions, and the suggestion that the only answers to them stand on shaky territory, leaves him feeling refreshed, a little more confident. Perhaps he doesn't need to worry too much about the future after all.

He plucks up the courage to speak
"But in your story Isobel is ..."

" ... an adult. And she was an adult when she was a child. She had always been better educated, more confident, to the point where she took it for granted that she knew what she was talking about (that was singularly the most annoying thing about her!). And I suppose it is all right if you belong to that metropolitan elite – that is, if you are on the educated, intelligent, mature, professional side of the divide. But what if you are not? What are you? Are you an experiment gone wrong? An imperfect prototype for something else? What if you are a child? What if you are a 'dumb' animal? What if you were an illiterate from the seventh century? What if you are elderly and your faculties are fading? You see: the idea of maturity – of adulthood – legitimises all kinds of wickedness."

David is not sure he has grasped everything clearly, but the man's evident passion gives David the impression that the man is on his side. He feels buoyed up, encouraged to believe in himself, and to take some faith in his view that the world of adults is not everything it is cracked up to be.

This leaves him to ponder freely the relationship of all these ideas to the origins of the lighthouse. Many unanswered questions remain in his mind, and he plays host to several areas of confusion so unformed that he cannot even formulate the question he can't answer.

The man, in his usual eerie way, anticipates David's thoughts. His eyes roll serenely over the surface of his young interlocutor, scanning for embodied signs of mental activity.

"I am sorry, David. We have strayed off the point a little. I have tried to educate you using the history of the lighthouse; and it must, at this point, seem unclear how any of this relates to that history. But I want to ask you to persevere with me. We are filling out a picture, stroke by stroke, even if I have indulged in one or two tangents along the way.

'My story is about to take a turn, and it may seem – given everything I have just said – like an *unconvincing* one. I have, in effect, set things up to take this turn."

"But it is really convincing?"

"Well, perhaps not. Some of the twists and turns I have already made are pretty unconvincing; and, let's face it, some things howl out with improbability. And, I have to say, I don't think I am going to become any more convincing. But I don't want to steer you too closely to an interpretation of what I have been telling you. You must, in the end, make up your own mind."

These comments are only the latest in a growing list of things that the man has said, which David does not completely understand. It is in these moments that David feels most frustrated and wants to shout out, "Why can't you just explain it to me clearly?! I still resort to picture books!"

The force of gravity seems to have an inordinate effect on David's forehead.

"Were you giving me a clue?" he asks

"It was a kind of clue. I don't want to make it too easy for you."

"I don't find it easy," says David. "I find it hard."

"I suppose that is to be expected."

"But if you expect that," he replies, piecing together the contradiction, "how can you expect me to understand?"

"Naturally, it is a fair point."

"Well …?"

"You are saying that you are not old enough to understand any of this – am I right?"

"That's right."

"But, I suppose, if you recognise that you don't understand, then that might mean you will begin to understand."

"Might it?"

"It might. And if it might mean that, then it might also mean that you don't need to get too worried about not rooting these things too firmly in the realms of the probable."

"Okay …"

"I should continue with the story."

David is reluctant to hear more, given that his brain has been turned inside out and washed on a high heat. He shrugs his shoulders.

"Right," continues the man, "brace yourself …

'I'll return to the third time I met Isobel in London. One evening I was in *The Bullfinch*. You remember I told you that the owner of my flat worked for the metropolitan police force. He said he did a 'spot of administrative work' for them. Well anyway, one evening, not too long after the party, I had arranged to meet Isobel for an evening bite to eat."

VIII

"The fourth time I met Isobel in London was the last. She came around – uninvited – to my flat. It had been raining, and some of the moisture seemed to have found the fringes of her hair. She stood before me. She looked at me with a hardness that disguised what she was really thinking.

'I escorted her into my cramped sitting room. She took off her raincoat. I offered her a cup of tea.

'"So," she said as I offered her a steaming cup, "I haven't seen you for a while. I was wondering what you have been up to."

'I sat carefully on the opposite side of the room.

'"Oh, not much," I said. "Just stuck in my usual routine."

'She nodded.

'"I just thought I would come around," she said.

'I smiled.

'"Good to see you," I said. "How have *you* been?"

'"Busy," she replied straight off. "Yes, very busy. I might be flying out to Italy – for a story," she explained. "I really came around ..."

'I could see she was trying to get something off her chest.

'"Yes?" I asked.

'She turned it back on me.

'"Can you not guess why I might have come round?" she asked.

'I looked at her. I remember I looked at her long and hard.

"'Well, it has been a few weeks since we last met, so I suppose it must have something to do with that. You didn't like my landlord, did you?" I asked.

"Do *you* like him?"

'I evaded the question.

"'He's my landlord," I replied.

'She shook some of the moisture from her hair.

"'I didn't like him, no. I can be quite *clear* about that."

'I tried to defend him.

"'I don't think he meant any harm."

'She hit back.

"'How can you say that? You of all … given your background … he's a pompous old fool!"

'I gulped.

"'Like I say, I don't think he meant any harm."

'Her eyes searched about me.

"'Have you … you know, I was always brought up to repay kindnesses. I don't want to flatter myself, but I have tried to, well, make life a little easier for you here in London. But so far I haven't really had much response from you. I have no idea what you think about me. The first two times we met, you said very little, and what you did say came across to me as perfunctory rather than sincere. And I just wonder … I am not actually being critical, but I wouldn't know of what I *could* be critical.

"A person must have opinions. They must stand for something. You must have some opinions surely? You have a brain – clearly you have a brain. You can see what goes on around you. So, use it to form some kind of conviction, *any* conviction.

"And the fact that I have not heard from you all this time – did it not occur to you that your landlord might have offended me? Did it not occur to you that our last meeting might have created some sort of atmosphere between us?"

"I stared at the carpet.

"'I am asking you, Sonny! That's a question!"

'I raised my eyes from the carpet.

"'I am sorry if I offended you. I didn't think anything I might think mattered that much."

'She gasped.

"'What *do* you think?" she asked.

'I stayed perfectly still.

"'About what?" I asked.

"'About *anything*," she replied.

'She took a moment to let this question sink in.

"'I mean, what do you do with yourself?" she went on, getting carried away with her own anger. "You have time, don't you? You read the newspapers. You talk to people. You *do* talk to people, I take it? Look around you. God knows there are enough social and political issues confronting just this country, never mind further afield. What about the Far East, and Africa? These are social realities. And they are crying out for our attention. So who are you? Where's your conscience?"

"Did she really say that?"

"Why? You don't believe me?"

"Well, it's not that. It just sounds a bit ..."

"Melodramatic?"

"What does that mean?"

"Over the top."

"Yes, I suppose."

"Yes, it was a bit, wasn't it. I was getting carried away. It was a serious moment, though don't you think? One in which I was right to get carried away?"

"Maybe."

"It was starting to get quite tense really, wouldn't you say? In some ways really quite dramatic."

"Maybe."

"She had asked a lot of questions. And okay, she may not have asked me about my conscience. But that was the spirit of the scene (we are painting with broad brush strokes).

'I would have liked to have answered her questions, but at that stage I didn't know how to answer them. The more she kept talking, the more guilt made it harder to think what the answers might be. I was crumbling under her gaze.

"'I don't know what I think," I said eventually.

'She tried to conceal a look of dismay, but a frown got the better of her intention."

Robert Stewart

light

I

On his third visit to the lighthouse David is swept by squally showers that come in sudden bursts. The water, cut and finely ground by the wind, whips against the side of his face, and waves thick locks of hair over his scalp.

Positioned in his now customary way before the journey along the peninsula, David looks like a physiological illustration of yin and yang: one side dry, the other wet; one cheek red raw from the needling rain, the other unblemished; one trouser leg dark, damp and redolent of seasonal change, the other unspoiled by the rain and still drowsy with the faded summer. Unpredictable gusts of wind gather over the open sea and make strategic skirmishes over the land, buffeting and jouncing the grip his legs have over the ground beneath him.

The weather is only the continuation of a low front that has hung over his part of the country for the last five days. So far it has kept him confined to his bedroom, to the TV, and to a set of wooden bricks which he uses to build elaborate structures and then demolish. This means that the weather has also strictured his education; he knows that bad weather means he is not allowed out, and certainly not allowed to brave the perils he might face along the peninsula. In this kind of weather, who knows what will emerge from the water. But as the days draw out, and the poor weather refuses to relent, the first day at his new school gets closer; and the closer this day gets the more it heightens the need to meet for a third lesson with the lunar-faced man in the lighthouse. His need to see the man increases almost in direct proportion to his mounting anxieties about life at his new school.

Now that the last day of the holidays has finally arrived, he no longer has a choice. This is his last opportunity. So he has decided that, even if it means rebelling against the rules of his household, he will pedal out to the lighthouse, in defiance of the wind and rain as they try to repel him.

He is confident that this time he will be the only human on the peninsula besides the man. There can surely be no-one else foolhardy enough to go out in this weather. Besides there is nothing to see. The nests and sedges have swallowed up all the birds, and the cloud and rain besmirch the horizon so that seafaring vessels are scarcely visible. And sex in the sandy undergrowth just isn't an option on a day like this.

This certainty that he will be alone with the curlicue of land stretching out into the mouth of the estuary is welcoming. People, in whatever comical incarnation, only drift around the peninsula as incongruous tourists wearing the signs of the culture and community they inhabit. The unforgiving landscape makes these few adventurers to the edge of civilisation stand out, and gives them the appearance of alien beings landing for the first time on an uninhabited and uninhabitable planet. To travel out to the lighthouse when the land is deserted and lashed by the rain, means that he is bearing the brunt of its true nature. Something else occurs to him: if it is raining, then the man may invite him inside the lighthouse.

He pulls down on the fastener attached to the hood of his cagoule, so that it won't blow free as he is cycling. He throws his legs over the bicycle, puts his head down and sets off.

Rattled by the wind and rain, he doesn't notice much until he reaches the collapsed stretch of road, where, as usual, he stops, dismounts and wheels his bicycle into the sandpit, descending once again a little closer to the waters underneath. If, as he imagines, the land sits on the water like the crust of skin on the surface of rice pudding, it seems likely that the land would move about more than it appears to, or even break free from the mainland and drift aimlessly out to sea. Frightening as this thought is, the prospect of drifting around the world's oceans on a bit of dismembered land with only the man and his lighthouse is exhilarating; they might sail from country to country, mooring wherever the currents deposit them, and attract visitors from the indigenous population. David envisages exotic women in grass skirts offering him consecrated coconuts, mangoes and other unusual fruit, and then dancing provocatively by the light of an open fire. He sees a crocodile of saffron-robed Buddhist monks marching up to the door of the lighthouse to receive alms and discuss great truths with the old man, like whether cranial girth has any bearing on intelligence, or if it is just the sign of an inflated brain.

As often happens when his mind wanders in this way, he catches himself doing it. His awareness that his thoughts are unhinged from reality creates the temporary sensation that someone has pulled a rug out from beneath him. For a moment he just stands on the collapsed road, looking over the river, and inland at the industrial plants sending out their carefully modulated tendrils of combustion. But this sight – the landscape of flat, rain-whipped water, lapping meekly at the edges of cargo cans, shuttling stevedores, and the web of grimy machinery – does nothing to yoke his thoughts. Whether it is the river, the harbour, or the open sea, there is nothing to supersede or correct his imagination. The peninsula, for better or worse, has no organised rules, code of conduct, or even the most primitive signs of civilisation. Everything stands, quite literally, on shifting sands.

He sways slightly in the wind as he looks over the estuary; the pulse of his mind has skipped a beat, or maybe several beats, and, without knowing it, he is waiting for its syncopated rhythm to begin again. He shuffles about in the sand. He sinks a little deeper, so that the sand has covered the tips of his Wellington boots. How much further down can it be before he hits the water? And will the ground simply give way completely, or will it become progressively more infirm, descending into a quagmire?

David is disturbed by a sound. There are more movements in the grass. But this time they are not clumsy or blubber-bottomed, but stealthy and svelte. A streak of tinged ginger trots out from the grasses and stands where the road picks up again. It stands very calmly before him, with no sense of aggression, surprise, or any detectable reaction of any kind. Even the feather-duster tail conveys no emotion.

The fox looks at him directly, without blinking an eye, without shifting a muscle. David remains similarly unmoved, but on the inside he is fighting off a spasm of fear. He has never been taught to be frightened of foxes, but he knows they can be aggressive; he knows they are scavenging vermin, and certainly not to be regarded in the same way as the domesticated creatures he has encountered at home. Even so, he doesn't think the fox will attack him, and the evolutionary stakes are stacked in his favour. In reality *he* is the predator, which means that the balance of intimidation and fear should lie in his favour.

There can be no doubt that the fox has seen him. It cannot, for example, have mistaken him for a small tree or an oddly discarded mannequin. It must know he is real. David demonstrates that he is real by moving his arm a little. This is not man at his most atavistic and barbarous, but it makes David look more threatening than if he were made of cardboard. The fox doesn't stir. It is unruffled by David's (tentative) assertion of natural superiority. He moves his arm back to where it was.

He knows that he cannot break eye contact with the fox. They are playing the staring game, and, even though they are species apart, a universal rule applies: the first to break eye contact has lost. Or so David thinks. The longer he stares at the fox, the more he has the sense that there is no bone of contention between them. Try as he might, he cannot detect anything in common, even mutual ill-will.

Time stretches out, far longer than it should. David senses that something unusual is at play. By this stage the fox ought to have bowed its head and slid silently back into the grasses, having disdained this feeble example of mankind's sovereignty over nature. But it remains.

David thinks about a more daring gesture. He could, for example, raise his fist to the fox, or better still, stamp his foot at it and shout, 'Be off with yer! Grrr!" in a way that he imagines people of a different generation spoke to scavenging animals. But he is not confident that he could deliver a 'grrr!' with anything like the required conviction, and if he were to try, he would just cut a cunning smile across the jaws of the creature.

This is, he thinks, the reality with which he must contend. The fox took one look at him, and peered straight into his soul. It saw him for what he is. It knows that David worries about pretty much everything. It can see through to his quivering yellow belly, and whatever menacing exterior David might try to assume, the fox will not be foxed. This must be the reason why it has not turned away. It is holding David prisoner. He is a captive of his own cowardice and general fear of being eaten by other animals.

There are others he knows who would definitely not have this trouble, who would not have given it this much thought. There are others who would have run the fox into the undergrowth or charged at it with maniacal war-whoops and military indifference. He knows a female sous chef with a hairy upper lip, who would go at it with a carving knife.

But this is not David's style, and the fox knows it. David doesn't carry an emergency sachet of seasoning in his back pocket.

He is suddenly irritated by the fox, as though its attempt to expose his inadequacies as a human being is somehow unkind and ungentlemanly. If the fox were at all compassionate, he thinks, it would simply mind its business, satisfied that the only human being stupid enough to brave the dangers of a rain-swept afternoon on the peninsula is not either a natural born hunter or a taxidermist keen to seize the moment.

David takes time out to think about things before he gets carried away with his rash judgements. Is there a bigger picture here, or a different way of looking at things? What, it suddenly occurs to him, if there is something behind him? What if there is more to this than meets the eye?

Carefully, in a way that suggests he doesn't trust the fox out of his sight, he looks quickly over his shoulder. Nothing stands behind him. Or, at least, nothing unusual. There is no brood of chickens or a beach-bound stray sheep. There isn't even a rabbit or a seagull. This means there can be no doubt about it. The fox is only interested in him. But what it is about him that has fascinated the fox quite so much and for so long, he really cannot understand. Is the fox trying to challenge him? Is it expecting him to attack? Is it waiting for him to run away? Is it frozen with fear?

The questions keep coming, and his fanciful answers to them could put considerable time between the present and his arrival at the lighthouse. But for some reason, the chattering noise of his mind begins to recede into the background, and the two creatures stare at each other calmly. Rather than a complete thought, or an attempt to make sense of the situation, he sees the fox in different scenarios. He sees it wandering here and there, trying to make good, stealing furtively – always a foreigner and an outsider – behind the backs of the civilisations on which it preys. Considered as a creature always at odds with its environment, it looks at home on the peninsula in an environment at odds with itself.

David opens his mouth, as if to speak to the creature, but it slips away before he can say anything.

II

'One of the only people I visited in the short remaining time that I stayed in London was my landlord. He had previously been someone I had always tried to avoid, but I remember I went to his apartment one evening.

'He opened his door.

'"Good evening," he said.

'He was drunk.

'"Good evening," I replied.

'He reached out and patted me on the shoulder.

'"Good evening. So it's you. So it is. Yes, indeed," he said.

'"Good evening," I repeated.
'"Yes. Indeed ... well, do come in, please."
'I walked into his apartment.
'There were lots of books and a number of paintings, some photographs. They looked like stills from films but I couldn't recognise from what films. In his living room, he invited me to sit down on his chaise longue.
'"Put your feet up; go on — please do. That's what it's there for. We don't stand on ceremony here. No. For starters there isn't enough room," he quipped.
'I sat on his chaise longue and he offered me a glass of wine.
'We talked; I asked how he was and so on.
'"I came around to apologise, really," I managed to slip in.
'My landlord swirled his drink in his glass. The glasses were small and Parisian.
'"There is no need for that," he said quite seriously. "No need at all. We live in a city. Full of many different people. You and I — I am sure we are very different. Of course we are different — I am a good deal fatter! Ah ha! And older ... No need for that at all. The seasons change. Water gushes under the bridge. Everything is impermanent, as they say in some quarters of the orient.
'Besides for what do you have to be sorry? And if you are looking to purchase a little redemption with your 'sorry's I must leave you with a pocket full of pennies, because — to reiterate — there is no crime.

And with no crime there is no criminal to which it can be traced. One word is derived from the other.

'So, you see, this worry-warting attitude of mind – it has no foundation. The subject of the sentence obtains only in your mind. This is a will-o'-the-wisp. Which somewhat undermines the reason for your visit, I should say. Of course, it would be nice to think that neighbours might pay each other visits out of good cheer and common-or-garden cordiality. But we have to be realistic. This is London. And I am your landlord.

'One cannot be liked by everyone, I suppose. To be liked at all is something."

'He let the thought diffuse, like smoke from an extinguished candle.

'"Yes, I agree," I said.

'My landlord looked at me long and hard. And then he chuckled inwardly.

'"Look at you, all tightly strung with the anxieties of ... I don't know much about you (we haven't really jawed) but even on the first day we shook hands and came to our little gentleman's agreement, I should have said that you look out of place. And my opinion hasn't changed. And, if I am candid, I should say you would look out of place anywhere. You are a portrait. Not a landscape. Could you pass the stuffed vine leaves?"

'I passed him a bowl on the coffee table.

'"Of course, you have an unusually round face. That doesn't help."

'I nodded.

'"Yes, I do have a very round face."

'He was grinning at my round face.

'"You sort of don't know where it begins or where it ends."

'I nodded again.

'"Yes, I do have a very round face."

'"They could use you in mathematical experiments," he added.

'He laughed out loud, which choked up a ruckle in his chest and caused a fit of coughing.

'"It perhaps takes one to know one," he said.

'"To know what?" I asked.

'"To know a misfit," he replied.

'"A misfit?" I said.

'"That's right; a misfit," he confirmed.

'"A misfit ..." I mused.

'"It takes one to know one," he repeated.

'"Uh huh," I said.

'"Not that being a freak is something you should be ashamed of," he added.

'"No?" I asked.

'"Good heavens, no. That wouldn't do at all. I mean plenty of other people will encourage you to feel that way anyway; you may as well show some pride. Though, in so doing, I suppose it only enhances or confirms the impression that you are ... that you are ..." he tailed away.

'"... a freak," I completed.

'"That's exactly what I was going to say," he said cheerfully. "Have a stuffed vine leaf."

'I fingered the bowl.

'"Thank you," I said.

'"But no," my landlord continued, "it's not just your unusually round face that's the problem. There's something more than that. I mean physical deformities are rife. You only have to look at some of the poor mutated creatures that assemble in London's less respectable drinking establishments. Or take a walk around King's Cross. There are some peculiarly shaped people in England, don't you think? I have always thought that the English look, well, a little unusual. England is not so much a garden of paradise as God's cabbage patch. But to bring it back ..." he searched for his thought, "to where I start... what was I saying?"

'I interrupted him.

'"Yes, what were you saying?" I asked.

'"Well, I'll tell you," he said. "I was going to say that it seems to me that there is something more. You're not just a young man with a freakishly round face. You ... how should I say? There are people one encounters – and they are at ease with their environment. But you are not. Your brain is all the time ticking furiously but quietly, observing extraneous circumstances, recognising a kind of inescapable difference from them. In fact, I would say that you don't like them."

'My landlord let me think.

'"Something came home to me recently," I said eventually.

' I explained that growing up to realise that I had been ignorant as a child and that I was – allegedly – no longer ignorant as an adult did not make me happy. In fact it made me the opposite. It made me unhappy.

'My landlord thought for a while.

"*Childlike, I danced in a dream;
Blessing emblazoned that day;
Everything glowed with a gleam;
Yet we were looking away!*"

"'Right,'" I said, nodding my head like a patient politely unconvinced by a session of quackish counselling.

"'Now let me see,'" continued my landlord. "You were happy as a child, and now you are an adult, you realise that you were ignorant as a child; but your realisation that you were ignorant as a child makes you unhappy. So, as a child you were happy but ignorant; but as an adult you are unhappy but educated."

'I nodded.

"'Something like that,'" I said.

'My landlord surveyed the paradox.

"'I suppose you can't have everything. But do you know what I would say?"

'I asked him what he would say.

"'I would say that you look like a freak and that you think like one."

'I confessed.

"'I was interested by what you said. That time in *The Hatch*."

'He sighed.

"'Yes, I see. Like I say, it would be nice to think that the young pay visits to their elderly neighbours out of the kindness of their hearts."

'I apologised.

'"I'm sorry," I said. "I was curious."
'He continued.
'"So we come to the crux of the matter. You did not come to apologise; even *that* was a pretext."
'I frowned.
'"No, no, I *did* come to apologise. I felt bad. But I also wanted to understand why. I thought you might be able to help me. I don't fully understand why."
'My landlord was pleasantly surprised by this.
'"Sort of like a teacher and his pupil, you mean?"
'I wasn't completely comfortable with this.
'"Perhaps," I said.
'"Well now, I suddenly feel in a position of authority; ready to flex my muscles of exposition."
'I challenged him.
'"Okay, explain it to me then," I said.
'"All right," he said, "I'll give it a good solid bash. But do give me a prod with a blunt instrument if I start off on some inebriated ... you get the picture."
'I said I would.
'"The problem seems to be ignorance, as though there were some sort of rule which says that happiness in a state of ignorance is a sham – bogus happiness."
'My landlord laughed.
'"One can only be truly happy when one is not ignorant. But suppose the premise that adults are not ignorant is wrong. I mean, it only takes its cue from the relative ignorance of children (talk about not picking on someone your own size). Does that mean there can never be genuine happiness? That all happiness is bogus? Or does it mean that the foundations upon which 'sensible', university-educated *citoyens* make

their judgements are not actually as firm as they might like you to think? Or even only as entrenched as their arrogance?

"So if all adults are in some way ignorant, that poses a challenge. Because it means that in many different ways, certain things will be unfamiliar, if not completely unknown. Take me, for example: I belong to a certain culture, and I come from a certain background – I recognise that much. I am also of a certain age. For those that come from a different background or are of a different age, that poses a challenge. Because, though not completely ignorant, they are not as familiar with my circumstances, just as I am ignorant of theirs. And take you: you look peculiar. You stand out. You are different. That poses a challenge too. There is a degree of ignorance that stands between you and others unlike you.

"Some of the challenges to ignorance I have already mentioned, might be construed as relatively trivial. Despite them, you and I and others we encounter in the latter half of twentieth century England, have more in common with each other than we do with the Zhou dynasty Chinese. So that degree of mutual ignorance – across time and culture – poses an even greater challenge.

"Not that it is beyond the circumspection of man to resolve some differences; but other differences seem to me to be insoluble. You could say that thought and language are unique characteristics of human beings, and in that sense instruments for the creation of some kind of division. And if the instrument for resolving the problem is itself part of the problem, then it means that some areas of ignorance will always remain. The challenge becomes greater still.

"And how do you answer that challenge? It seems to me that there are two ways: you either respect it or you don't. You can kid yourself that you aren't ignorant; you can claim to be an 'adult', and claim a bogus authority. Or you can strike your pose, overcoming ignorance where possible, but knowing and accepting that, so to speak, your pose will be mysterious to the Zhou dynasty Chinese.

"So bringing it back to your paradox, if all adults are in some way ignorant (and I can't believe this premise is that controversial), then we can infer a perspective from which all adults in a sense look and behave 'like children'.

"I suppose you could say, then, that we have come full circle."

III

No lights are on inside the lighthouse, and splinters of daylight manage to squeeze around the edges of the boarded-up windows. Peering in through the open door makes it even harder, as the contrast between the opaque interior and the visible exterior makes it harder for his eyes to adjust.

He knows that the threshold will be hard to cross. As with everything about the man in the lighthouse and his successive 'lessons', there is a note of caution at the back of his mind taught to him either by the instructions of his parents or an instinct for survival. Each visit, each encounter with the man, the note sounds a thin, reedy voice, piping feebly against the choral crescendo of his naked curiosity. However feeble, the conflict creates in him a rising panic, which must resolve into a decision.

David has a premonition that as soon as he has crossed the threshold, the door will close behind him, and he will be trapped in the dark, at the mercy of a sinister plot. These considerations, these natural – though in some ways irrational – fears, David must weigh up against everything he stands to gain; but when judged in this way, he is still not sure of the advantages, or if the prize of 'an education' pearls with anything like the glory that would justify a decision to drag his drenched body one step further.

He thinks of a conversation he held with his parents not more than a week ago, in which he had inadvertently let slip the preoccupations that have kept him out of their hair in the run up to the end of summer.

"Why do you never buy muffins?" he had asked.

They had asked him why he wanted to know why they never bought muffins.

He had replied that the man who lives in the lighthouse had offered him a muffin.

Their faces had turned Antarctic with terror.

"David," his mother had said, "no-one lives in the lighthouse. Who was this man?"

He had managed to wriggle out of it by keeping his eyes fixed on the floor, and explaining that he had meant Reginald, the man in the caravan park from whom he had acquired his bicycle.

"I've started calling him 'the man who lives in the lighthouse'," he had explained.

"Why?".

David had thought for a while.

"I don't know."

The tower of the lighthouse sucks the rain into the circular orbit of its tower as he relives this memory; and, without another thought, he walks into the darkness.

Against his expectation, the door stays open behind him, and the shafts of daylight that peer around him still make it difficult to see anything inside the lighthouse. He walks in a little further, carefully so as not to collide with a concealed table or a surreptitiously planted armchair.

His eyes begin to adjust. Shapes form in the room. He sees the foot of a spiral staircase only a few steps away, swirling into the ceiling, like a free ride to the Land of Oz. A bucket lies at the foot of the wall immediately opposite him, and above, a rivulet of damage has been carved into the wall, descending from the boarded-up window. He thinks he can see traces of moisture on the wall, and beads of water sweating inside the rivulet. The air in the room is damp and cold. This room, he thinks, surely can't be inhabited.

"Hello," he calls out, but his voice is stillborn in the stagnant air.

He walks across to the foot of the staircase, and peers upwards. There is no obvious light on the floor above.

"Hello," he calls up the flight of stairs, this time a little louder.

There is no answer.

Perhaps he ought to turn back. Surely, if the man were inside the lighthouse, he would have heard him calling, and answered. There is now no good reason to go any further. To have come this far might be construed as acceptable given that he and the man have met before, but to explore the lighthouse while the man is not there amounts to trespassing on his property. If he climbs the first flight of stairs and someone else finds him in the lighthouse – a stray policemen, for example – he will, almost certainly, be hauled up before the local magistrate, and maybe even sentenced to a short but formative term in an institution for young offenders, where young boys with a rheumy darkness about the eyes will take pleasure in smashing his knee-caps with snooker balls. They will force him to endure further ignominies by stripping him to his underpants, encircling him and forcing him to make like a crippled monkey. Already he wishes he had never been born.

But, even now, there is still a dilemma; and it is the same dilemma, distilled and finely ground. If he turns back, that will be it. This is his last opportunity to meet with the man before his secondary education – which is now only a matter of hours away – begins. And in spite of everything he has so far learned, and in spite of no condition which says that whatever he is going to learn, he must learn now, he wants to see the man today. This day feels like his last opportunity. Beyond today, he is sure that something will change. And once it changes his incipient, as-yet-uninfluenced mind will be less susceptible to the man's message. On the far side of the day's coming-to-pass there stand officious teachers, a schooling in ill-informed but peremptory judgement, drug abuse, smoking, a certain attitude to haircuts, terminal, transcendental humiliation, and, more than anything, an army of meat-headed morons ready to unload their socially disaffected violence on his skull. Then, of course, there is his simple curiosity about the 'light' in the lighthouse.

David begins to climb the stairs.

The second floor is even darker than the first. There is no open door, and no daylight to flood the room. The only light available streams upwards from the floor below. But the light is so thinly spread that its impact is negligible, and has no obvious impact on the blackness of the room. By groping about with his hand, he can just about feel the upward spiral of the staircase.

"Hello," he calls out, again, louder and braver still.

But the air's refusal to carry sound mimics the intensification of his efforts.

By the time he reaches the third floor, daylight has started to infiltrate the room from the opposite end of the building. Passing over the third floor – which seems, like the other floors, to have little or no content – he scurries up the next flight of stairs to what must be the room penultimate to the watchtower. The staircase ends here. He steps out over a yellow carpet, faded and threadbare (with a faint smell of fish). The room is more hospitable, but even so, it contains no furniture. A plastic kettle squats uncomfortably on a wooden tray, adjacent to a socket in the wall. A bean bag, hollowed and thrust against the wall, rests at arm's length from the kettle. A couple of books are piled up at the opposite end of the room. The only other feature is a ladder that ascends through the ceiling into the room's only source of light.

"Hello," he calls out again, but uncertainty has crept back into his voice, and the noise he makes sounds feeble and without purpose.

David walks around the room a little, slightly panicked by the sense that the higher he gets the more illicit his activity becomes. For trespassing only as far as the second floor, a judicious magistrate with a sense of perspective might have let him off with a warning, but now that he has more or less climbed to the top of the lighthouse, a gruesome end awaits. And there is nowhere to hide. He thinks momentarily about how he might assume the guise of a wall, or a particularly convincing statue of a child. But one way or the other, he would jar with his surroundings. If the egg-shaped head of the local constabulary were to investigate this far, they would catch him red-handed, and in a slightly smug and self-congratulatory way, remark 'Hullo, what have we here?', like a big game hunter settling confidently on their prey.

Like the hubristic intrigues in history and its great tyrants, David has come so far that the tedium of his return has no power over his vertical study of the building.

Quickly, in order to prevent fate from snatching his prize away from him when it is only within a clammy palm's reach, he scales the ladder and emerges into the glass bowl at the head of the building.

The man, he sees, stands at the other side of a peculiar object in the centre of the room that looks like a recreation in miniature of the room in which he is standing; and inside the miniature he thinks he can see another miniature. He almost expects to find a scaled-down version of himself, studying his own study of himself.

The impression of the man through the glass is a mixture of splintered, convex and concave distortions, so that each slight movement he makes has a broad range of unpredictable repercussions for the way he appears.

"Hello," the man says.

David straightens in the presence of the man, who, somehow at the heart of the lighthouse, assumes a faintly changed manner that is no longer outward-looking, no longer casting his net wide in search of pupils to educate, but confident that they will come slithering out of the ocean into his arms.

"How are you today?" he asks.

David stares a little warily at the man.

"It's quite wet," he says.

"So it seems," says the man, looking David up and down.

"I am sorry; I have been waiting for it to stop. But it hasn't stopped. Mum and dad – they don't like me going out in the rain."

"That's understandable. So what's changed?"

David looks out of the window.

"Today is the last day of the summer holidays," he says.

"I see."

"I wanted to visit you before the holidays end. I thought that ..."

"... yes?"

"... I thought that if I didn't come before the end of the holidays, you might not be here."

The man doesn't say anything, which confounds David's expectation. Since there is no good reason why the man should abandon his watch at the end of the summer holidays, he expects his confession to be met with a patronising peel of laughter. The man's silence is ambiguous, and because it is ambiguous, it is unnerving.

"So you have braved the elements while there is still time."

"I suppose so," David replies.

"Well, we do have several loose ends, and given our original agreement, it would be fitting to tie them off before you put your blazer on for the first time. Is it tomorrow that it all kicks off?"

"Yes. Tomorrow."

"At what time?"

"I have to catch the bus at ten past eight. We're the second stop. I know some of the other people who get it. But not all. Not the older ones. But the older ones sit at the back of the bus. That's what my friends say anyway."

"The great chain of being contains many different hierarchies."

"I'm happy at the front of the bus. Near the driver."

"Uh huh. Who knows, one day you may become more ambitious."

"I doubt it."

"Are you nervous? About tomorrow?"

David stops to think.

"Yes," he admits.

"Okay, well in that case, before the sentence is carried out, we should perhaps give you something to think about when you are steaming up the window on the bus."

"Yes, I would like that," says David quietly.

"My impression from our previous meetings has been that your thoughts have been gradually finding a momentum, and I am half-expecting this lesson to contain challenges for both of us."

"Yes, I have been thinking about your story. I have some questions. I have been creating a list of them. In my head."

The man walks around the watchtower, peering into its mechanical nucleus.

"Not that I want to discourage your questions, but my story is nearly but not quite complete. There are just a few final things to say. And since there is a chance that the story in its entirety might pre-empt the answer to some of your questions, then it seems only fair and reasonable for me to complete it. Would you agree?"

David puts his hands in his pockets, like a businessman signalling agreement over a point of negotiation. Only real businessmen don't wear Wellington boots.

"Yes, I think so."

"Okay then. Now if I remember rightly," says the man, in a way that makes it more than possible that he hasn't, "I was in London the last time we met. Is that right?"

"Yes, that's right. You were in London."

"Yes, that's right. Of course I was. I was in London. But I wasn't there for long, you see. No. You might even say that I bolted. And I didn't really do much or see anyone after my meetings with Isobel. One of the only people I visited in the short remaining time that I stayed in London was my landlord. He had previously been someone I had always tried to avoid, but I remember I went to his apartment one evening."

IV

"What *is* the lighthouse?" he asks.

The man shuffles about uncomfortably on his feet, and then walks a few steps in one direction as though he were hoping to escape, but quickly realises that any walk will only take him back to where he started. Between the two of them and their conversation, the room is starting to feel hot.

"If you think back to our first lesson, you will remember that as a young man I had developed some strange ideas about circles, as though the geometry of a circle were a better representation of the mind's attempt to make sense of things than a straight line. Strange idea, I know. And if you think back to our second lesson, you will remember that, as I grew up, I naturally came to see that this was a strange idea. But now my landlord was telling me that the 'sober' perspective from which I was looking back on my silly ideas as a child was perhaps not as sober as I thought, and, in fact, from an imagined perspective, might be seen as every bit as silly as the silliness I saw in my younger self. This meant that I had gone from a silly child to a sober adult, and back to a silly child, or a child-adult (a 'chult', if you will). And because I had completed this circle, it lent more credence to my 'silly' ideas about circles.

'Of course, you might say that if my silly ideas about circles were not as silly as they at first seemed in retrospect, then there was nothing silly *at all* about being a child. But if that were the case, then the theory of circles would be wrong, which, in turn, would mean that I was silly as a child, so vindicating the theory ... to save us from the circularity, I'll cut it short there. You get the idea."

David doesn't get the idea. There are so many crossed wires in his brain that it is fast becoming a health and safety risk. He is starting to feel that the sudden onslaught of overlaid, inter-meshed thoughts that he is now trying to manage, is causing his mental circuitry to go soft and cease functioning as a conductor for any kind of thought. If someone were to drill into his head at this point, they would only find a heap of slightly soggy spaghetti. David entertains himself for a moment by moving his head from side to side to check if he can hear anything squelching about.

"So, there was an important conclusion. This kind of 'circular' logic meant that the principle of circularity was correct in some way, but that the perspectives from which, as both a child and an adult, I looked silly had to exist for it to be true (of course, in the case of a child, this perspective is an adult). The implications of that is a kind of mind-boggling infinitude. It suggests that there is no stopping-point; if, for example, you could enter into the 'perspective' from which as an adult you behaved with the relative maturity of a child, it suggests that there would, in turn, be another 'perspective' from which the first perspective would demonstrate the relative maturity of a child. And so on."

David's heart is beating fast, just as his brain is trying to work fast. But the discomfort this creates in him makes him long for a simpler time; a time in which he was innocent of the lighthouse and its strange meaning; and of the prospect of his secondary education and all the apparent damage it is about to inflict on him; and of all circuitous reasoning. If all education is this hard, David thinks that he is not cut out for the academic life, and that he should focus at an early stage on something more vocational, like window cleaning.

He likes bicycles, and he followed the work of his companion in the caravan park closely when he had assembled his bicycle. He enjoyed getting his hands dirty oiling the chain, and ensuring that the three-gear switch didn't dangle from his handlebars. He thinks he could, when he is mature, own a bicycle shop and oil other people's chains, mend their punctures, and provide expert ergonomic advice about seating. He imagines queues of grateful people with bent spokes and misaligned cross-frames coming to him for help and a comforting chat about the latest developments in shock absorption.

"So, there is another important conclusion," continues the man. "This kind of thought implies that there will always be a perspective from which you either — as in your case — are a child, or are 'like' a child. In some ways that could be a bit frustrating. Every time you successfully complete a crossword puzzle, or preside over a minor achievement at work, or even set out a compelling approach to quantum theory, it is as though some spiteful bureaucrat with a sour grin is assessing your achievements as no more noteworthy than a monkey successfully negotiating the skin off a banana after a doctoral period of study. And let's face it, that might leave you feeling a little piqued.

'Some people might get angry. Others subdued. Still others might rush out and fling themselves off the nearest suspension bridge. One way or the other, some kind of low front sets in. And you might even say that, if this particular academy of thought only fosters an outlook on life which hikes up the human rain under suspension bridges, has it really got that much going for it?"

David still thinks he is a child but is not sure. He is quietly confident that he is not an adult, but reticence is the safest option in the world that the man describes, where he may have unknowingly sired some exceptionally small progeny who look up to him as a paragon of good sense and worldly wisdom.

"Well of course it hasn't. But then you have to ask what motivates a suicidal plunge into the abyss? I'll put it simply: if you think you are big, but it turns out you are relatively small, that might leave you feeling a little disheartened. But if you recognise that you are not that big from the outset – that is if you have a firmer grasp on reality – then maybe it isn't so disheartening. In fact maybe it gives you the opportunity to behave in a way that befits your size. Despair, disillusionment and a morbid fascination with unhappy endings are, in this sense, just confounded arrogance. Or judgement with no sense of proportion or circumspection.

"To have that sense of proportion, in this case means thinking the unthinkable; thinking your way into a state where thinking itself becomes an object of study. And the only way to do that is to 'imagine' what it might be like. And to undertake a leap of the imagination you need an image with which to leap."

David is mulling over the man's words, his confidence teetering on the edge of restoration, as he dares to think he might have understood.

"That's the lighthouse, you mean?" he asks.

"That's right."

"So you are saying that the lighthouse is a leap of imagination?"

"In a sense."

"Not a way of warning ships about land?"

"No."

David finds this difficult to accept. It seems to him that he is step-stoning from one improbability to the next.

"Do you see what I am saying?" asks the man.

"Not really," David admits.

"Okay then. Okay. Let me try to explain. I am your teacher and you are my pupil – yes?"

"Yes."

"That relationship assumes that I know what I am doing, and, to some extent anyway, you don't."

"I suppose so."

"But though it might seem, from your perspective, that I am the fount of all knowledge, I will tell you freely now that I am not. My recognition of that limitation implies that there is a perspective from which I am the pupil and some unspecified other is the teacher. But the only relationship that is immediately available to me is the one in which I am the teacher; so I cannot 'see' the scenario in which I am the pupil as clearly as the one in which I am the teacher. This means I need some way of imagining what it might be like to be a pupil in a state of relative innocence. Using the 'image' of a teacher and his pupil is one way; using the images contained in the lighthouse is another. The only difference is that the imagery of the lighthouse is a better representation – a clearer image – with which to work."

This is hard work. David is still struggling. His understanding is not moving in a straight trajectory towards a full grasp of what the man is saying, but instead ranging arbitrarily in and out of proximity to this goal. It feels like the man is teasing him, which leaves David frustrated, a feeling that transposes easily into a more earnest, and slightly angry, will to understand. He thinks, nevertheless, that there is just too much for him to grasp. He is just too young, too uneducated at this stage in his life to stand even a remote chance. Each lesson has given him this feeling, and each lesson has stirred in him an appetite to overcome these limitations, not just to grow up physically, but to grow up intellectually. Perhaps when he is knocking his knees together in fear on the bus to his new school, some of the things that the man has been saying will fall into place. But not now.

"What is it?" asks the man.

"I don't ..." David says hopelessly.

"You don't understand why the lighthouse is a better image?"

"No ... no ... not even that. No matter how many times you try to explain it ... I just don't get it ..."

David wants to say that he is only eleven. He wants to say that it has not been much more than a blink of an eye since he learned to read, to think in any kind of ordered way, and to make basic calculations. It is not that long ago that he mastered the alphabet. And when he reads, his preferred books still have pictures in them. How, then, can the man expect him to understand these things?

The man senses David's anxiety.

"I think I understand. We talked about this last time, if I remember rightly. 'I am only eleven' you are secretly shouting at me. 'How can I hope to understand this?' We talked about this before – I am right, aren't I?"

"Yes. We did."

"Can you remember what I said on that occasion? I am not sure I can."

This seems unlikely to David, even though the man manages to sound sincere.

"You said that I should think about it. You said that if I don't understand then that would mean I might begin to understand."

"Well that makes sense, doesn't it?"

"Does it?"

"I am sure I was talking sense."

"Perhaps," says David doubtfully, and then with more courage, "but it doesn't make sense to me."

"But that's the point isn't it? Isn't that what I was trying to get you to understand?"

David swallows air as if to say "You tell me!"

"What have I been saying? Just now I mean."

David shifts his weight from one leg to the other as if to say "good question!"

"What do you know?" asks the man.

"Nothing," David blurts out.

"But even if you did know nothing – which you don't – you would know that you know nothing, and therefore know something."

"Uh huh," says David, struggling to quantify the emptiness in his brain.

"But the truth of the matter is that you know something more than nothing, but only enough to know that you know something more than nothing and not everything."

"Okay."

"You see, things are actually very clear for you."

"Right."

"Not only are you in the position where you can clearly see and feel your ignorance, by virtue of the fact that you are still a child, but you also have the benefit of a teacher who draws attention to your ignorance by confusing you with the endless complexities of its nature. Believe me, you're the lucky one!"

"Because I am a pupil, you mean?"

"Exactly. Well done."

David muses hard.

"So, what are you saying?" he asks.

"Yes, I can begin to see how this is not easy; and how third-period geometry in a post-1960s battleship-grey estate might, at this point, seem preferable. I can see that I need to claw one back from the comprehensive system of education.

'But what I am saying is that you should spare a thought for me. If only you think about it – as you have just done – you can get your bearings easily (or relatively easily). I have recourse to building lighthouses!"

David is now thinking that he has not placed the last few weeks of his childhood in the hands of a tutor capable of steering him sensibly through life, or even in the hands of a reclusive pederast hatching the most impossibly complex plot to corrupt the youth of a child yet conceived; instead David is thinking that he has signed over his innocence, lock, stock and barrel, to a half-baked fruitcake, someone who has only managed to escape sectioning by withdrawing to a remote part of the country where the dignitaries that decide such matters can scarcely discern a lunatic foaming at the mouth from an upstanding citizen. And caught between a bouncing buttock and a football-headed fugitive from the asylum, David thinks that his own journey towards adulthood must consequently be hampered from the start; and that he will, moreover, only wind up as another unhinged vagrant wandering across the dystopian metropolis of the modern world conversing in psychologically disaffected babble.

"And that's where you should count yourself lucky. And that's where my education comes into its own. Because the public sector wants to cheat you of everything you have at the moment – that clarity about your ignorance. They want to steal it from you, pillage it systematically, and give you the false impression that you are not ignorant. They want to educate you, the swine! And me? Be ignorant, I say! Understand it, photograph and frame it, before you lose sight of it altogether. Record the moment for posterity.

'It may seem to you at this point that the intellectual asphyxiation to which I am subjecting you is uncaring, unkind and horribly unfair; and it is – that is why it is caring, kind and fair, because you can at least see that it is uncaring, unkind and horribly unfair. *Now* do you see what I am saying?"

David wants to say 'yes' and 'no'.

"I want to say 'yes' and 'no'."

"Well then, I can sense my triumph over the national curriculum."

They bask in a moment of pause.

"I'll say it again," continues the man, "the lighthouse encourages me to put myself in a similar situation to the relationship in which you stand to me. And I could achieve that, I suppose, by using words, by conjuring up these images using only language. Some people, though they would be comparatively few, might even respond to my efforts. But many others would, I am sure, come away bewildered, or eye me only with the pity they reserve for solitary individuals who talk a little too much about the sacramental purpose of lighthouses. Still others couldn't care less. Literacy has been the privilege of an elite for the greater part of history; and even now state education, reading clubs and societies have only made a slight dent in that privilege.

'What about all the others? How should I get through to them? If you follow through my aims, all I am trying to do is find an image, something that will lodge in the mind and help imagine – you might even say "recall" – a lost perspective. To do that, the image has to be meaningful; and, sure, words are meaningful if you work hard enough at them. But if the purpose I have set myself is to create an image that challenges the polymathic posturing of the adult mind, the words have to be treated warily, since they are only the subordinates of the intelligence that rules them. And this means that even meaning has a borrowed "meaning". Not every living thing uses words, much less the English language. Monkeys, birds, dogs ... the animal kingdom generally, do not lose any sleep over the nominative and accusative cases or the syntactical flesh and blood grafted onto them."

David has an image of an obedient border collie, a goose and a hyperactive monkey perched at a row of desks trying to study the elliptical meaning of the lighthouse, but descending into a pecking, squawking, hissing, snarling punch-up with lots of teeth, fur and feathers. In this image, his mind finds it uncannily easy to substitute all the animals for children at his new school, with no appreciable difference in the degree of carnage or bestial resistance to the civilising influence of education.

"But a building, now there's something different. A building, unlike words, can become an object of curiosity. It may be more oblique, but it is only as oblique as anything (human or beast) that steals eyes on it."

David remembers something from one of their earlier lessons.

"What about the shipwreck? You can't have built that."

"No. That's true. But that doesn't mean it isn't part of the image."

"How did it ... get there?"

"Or what does it mean?"

"What do you mean 'what does it mean'? Isn't it a shipwreck?"

"Yes, but it is part of the scenery."

"Part of the story, you mean?"

"That's the implication."

David looks down at the shipwreck through the thick panes of glass.

"What *does* it mean?"

"In the end it's just a detail. Don't let it confuse you.

David wants to make it clear that his confusion about the details add up to near total confusion.

"I don't understand – did you travel up from London by boat or something?" he asks, only thickening the fog in his mind, "Why didn't you get the train? Are you against privatisation?"

This is a word that he has heard in connection with rail travel, but which he also doesn't really understand.

"Perhaps you are now like one of those young boys from the 1950s who is pulling the thread out of a knitted jumper. This is just my loose thread. Keep pulling. Perhaps it will all fall apart. Or perhaps it won't. Perhaps there is a meaning. But I will leave you to find it.

'Going back to the imagery of a teacher and his pupil (and I am going to mix up the images again) the "teacher" gets to a point where they realise that in some sense they are a "pupil". The teacher goes from thinking he is knowledgeable and clever to realising that he is relatively ignorant and stupid. But with the imagery of teacher and pupil, you can only ever be one or the other. This is the difference. With the lighthouse, you can be both."

"Both teacher and pupil?"

"Well, if you want to mix up the images ..."

Now that David is thinking about the images as images rather than as something real – even though the relationship in which he stands to the man and their current location are real instances of the images – he has the feeling that they are standing in the way of his understanding; and that there is a simpler and more precise way to explain this, using something clear, like mathematics.

"What the lighthouse says, which the imagery of the teacher and his pupil doesn't, is that at any one time I can be – in fact I am – from some perspective both a teacher and a pupil, that I am suspended between knowledge and ignorance, happiness and unhappiness, justice and injustice, beauty and ugliness ... I could go on. In one circumstance, I might be unhappy, treated unfairly, perceived as a lug-eared lamebrain, but take a trip round the corner, grow up, (maybe even die) and the perspective changes. The light keeps coming around again. And my point is that the lighthouse doesn't diminish the significance of its flashing torch but shows it for what it is. So it would be conceited to think that the comparatively small area that each circuit of the lighthouse illuminates amounts to a complete illumination. But it would be just as conceited to deny anything of any value in these illuminations, because it would imply that *only* a complete illumination is worth aspiring to. And that means, so to speak, that I can celebrate the trilling lyricism of my 'childish' mind, moving from one whimsy to the next, in full awareness and in spite of the fact that, in some sense, my naivety and innocence are absurd."

David tries to 'picture' the image of himself and his teacher, and aligns it closely to his image of the lighthouse. Once more he looks down through the misted glass at the distorted shape of the shipwreck.

V

David is watching the man suspiciously. A thought has occurred to him, but it is at the moment not yet fully formed, and still so unsure of itself that it might easily vanish in a display of self-doubt.

David's eyes are narrowing. They compress his vision of the man, so that he can see only the essential details of his appearance, and in particular so that he can home in on the movement of his lips. If he tries hard enough, David thinks that he might discern the trickery he now suspects, but which he cannot entirely bring himself to believe. He half expects a clue to escape from the man's mouth – an unwitting burp of disclosure.

The deception is not altogether clear. But there is now a loop to the story; and how the man has formed this loop makes David want to revisit his first and second lessons to remind himself of how it all happened. It makes him think that he has not paid close enough attention; and that the connecting pieces in the story have escaped his attention, as his mind wanders astray, distracted by the thoughtless provocations of food, fear, and intimate, non-attired parts of the human anatomy.

But chiefly it is the loop itself — even if David cannot see all the connections — that arouses his suspicion. He cannot immediately call to mind any one part of the man's story that seems inconsistent or obviously contrived. But in coming 'full circle' as the man's landlord in the story said, David thinks he can see a conceit. He thinks he can see a lie, planned in some detail, one that has wormed out inconsistencies, and created full-bodied characters to make it more complete, more contrived, a more practised and polished deception. The man has become as chimerical and untrustworthy as everything else about the peninsula.

A second layer of thought follows these suspicions, and changes the complexion of things still further. It seems uncharacteristic of the man, and the relationship in which David stands to him, for this to be an error through which David has seen. In fact the way in which the man has told the story suggests the opposite. It is as though the man has dressed up the contrivance specifically for the occasion, and is now parading it in full view of his beguiled audience. The man is drawing out David's suspicion deliberately.

If the contrivance is itself contrived, then David wonders to what effect. His eyes, narrowed by suspicion, begin to widen again, and through them he directs only curiosity.

"What is it?" asks the man, who sees the changing weather behind David's eyes.

David doesn't know where to begin. He is overwhelmed by too many questions and too much to think about.

He pauses, trying simultaneously to order his thoughts and get the full measure of his current circumstance. More than at any other point in his three meetings with the man, he now feels his whole body and mind, all the shambolic thoughts that have filtered through his delinquent brain, converge on this issue. He is so entirely committed to his education that it threatens to engulf and suffocate him. He knows he is at the threshold, but of what he is not quite sure.

"What? What is it?" the man repeats, almost laughing.

David feels pressed to say something, but wary of doing so.

"Nothing," he says, "it's just that I don't understand."

"Don't you?"

"I ... it's just," David falters, still demanding too much of himself.

"What don't you understand?"

David looks again into the peculiar centre of the lighthouse, from which he assumes the light emanates when the building is operational.

"It just seems ... well, a bit unlikely," he says.

"A coincidence, you mean?"

"Yes, I suppose."

"What's coincidental about it?"

"I mean ... why would your landlord say that ... about 'coming full circle'? It's like he was finishing off ... or like he knew what you had been thinking as a little boy."

"I was a teenager," replied the man, "and he did know what I had been thinking as a younger man. I had told him – were you not paying attention?"

"No, I was paying attention. I know that," David says hurriedly. "It's just that you didn't tell your landlord about the circles. You didn't say it like that."

"Didn't I? Well maybe I didn't relate everything exactly as it happened. Maybe I glossed over some of the details, skim-read some of the fine print. I am only human after all!"

David looks warily at the man again, as if this final plea is actually a tacit suggestion of the opposite: that the man in the lighthouse is not 'only human', but somehow inhuman or supra-human.

"I don't know," says David still more doubtfully, "it's like you ..."

"... like I what?" asks the man eagerly.

"... like you made it all up. Or parts of it anyway. All that stuff about your childhood, and your time in London."

The man grips the railing that runs at waist height around the inside of the watchtower.

"I'm sorry," David says, unsure if he means it.

"Let me try to re-assure you," continues the man. "I can see that I need to rebuild your faith in me. Do you know what happened to Isobel? Of course you don't. Well, I'll tell you. Her ambitions as a writer were never quite fulfilled. Her first novel met with a lukewarm response, and though she made repeated attempts to write others, she began to lose the will, and became more and more immersed in her journalism. She wrote article after article, broadening her base of contacts, developed ties with cutting-edge academics, playwrights and artists, and developed an impatient sense of moral outrage at the manifest injustices and back-door elitism in the British parliamentary system.

'In the end, she devoted all of her efforts to journalism, and became, in particular, something of an expert in the field of education. She scrutinised White Papers, took part in heated debates, formed close relationships with young and undaunted members of pressure groups, and lampooned and derided the unthinking speeches of reactionary politicians. And the last that I heard of her she was the educational correspondent for the *Manchester Guardian*. Isn't that interesting? You might even say 'ironic'. Imagine the kind of conversations we would have had ..."

"Have you seen her since London?" asks David, still trying to find his feet and treating this diversion as an opportunity to do so.

"No ... no, I haven't seen her since then. In any case, I somehow feel she would only swirl around me in a pashmina of disapproval."

"Uh huh," David says without really thinking.

"These are, I suppose, only small extra details, but they do round off my story about Isobel a little, don't you think? Does that re-assure you? Even if you doubt me, you have to agree that turning her into the educational correspondent for the *Manchester Guardian* is a fairly seamless evolution of her character. You can imagine ... or perhaps you can't. You're only young, after all."

"I've never read a newspaper," David admits.

"Ah hah!" the man chokes with laughter, and a smile cuts into his cheeks, drawing out the roundness of his face. "You don't sound re-assured!"

"No, I suppose I am not," says David, sensing his way through the conversation.

"And you would be right not to be," the man concedes. "I have to say that it is satisfying to see that you have listened, and – perhaps – that you have understood. You are quite right, David. Everything I have told you over the last few weeks was a fabrication; it was a lie. I made it up. All of it."

"All of it? Even about your childhood?"

"Yes. In fact I don't even have a childhood. It was all imagined."

"Why?"

"Can't you guess? I have suggested to you on more than one occasion that this was all fabrication. Surely it cannot be that much of a surprise. The answer lies in the story, after all. In fact it brings us back to where we started.

'More than once in the course of the last three meetings you have suggested to me that you are frightened of what might happen to you tomorrow and in the years that ensue. And I will repeat my injunction: *be* frightened. It *is* frightening. The world that awaits you is a world of clamouring answers. You will not be taught to think, only to learn. That is the measure of confidence with which so-called reality is flaunted. The act of finding something out does not presage an as yet unknown discovery, let alone entertain the idea of discoveries that must remain unknown. Education *has* no edges. It is *not* human.

'Or rather it is a human that has assumed the imagined deportment of a god. It is like a fat Roman empress powdering her flabby cheeks with pigments that would, to a different time and culture, look utterly ridiculous. And if the accounts of reality taught in classrooms are, in part anyway, a comical rouge doesn't that mean that in, equal part, all the facts that make up those accounts can be made to look like fictions? Stories, like children, contain the imperfection clearly: a fiction is necessarily false; a child necessarily immature. As images, they are home-grown produce on which the imagination can feed in order to get a sense of what its own fleeting nature and limitations might look like. They help assume the attitude of a temporary light projected into an overwhelming darkness."

"The lighthouse, you mean?"

"Exactly."

David, still muddled, thinks about the man's words for a moment.

"What *is* the lighthouse?" he asks.

VI

"There isn't really that much more for me to say to you. When I first saw you, I promised that I would offer you an alternative to your education. I said that I would teach you by example, and the example is the lighthouse. But I have now sketched out the contours of my example, and hopefully filled in some of the detail.

'Our third lesson is over, and I think I have said everything I have to say. Autumn approaches. The nights draw in. Summer school is over.

'I hope you think these lessons have been productive. I have certainly enjoyed your company. As you might imagine, I don't get to see many people. Sometimes I see tiny midget-like figures wandering around at the foot of the peninsula, but very few summon the effort to come all the way out here. Which leaves me to wander alone in and out of the lighthouse amid the marram grass and the gulls. Perhaps this is why I have talked so much, and have not really given you a proper opportunity to chip in. I haven't meant to stifle you. Too much time alone only damns up your words, syllable by syllable, phonic by phonic, letter by letter. And when the dam is breached, an inevitable effusion follows.

'It wouldn't surprise me at all if, at the end of these lessons, not everything is clear. That is permitted. It is even encouraged. This is one of the main features that set my curriculum apart from others. Little by little. Piece by piece. Each according to his own.

That is my approach. And I don't dish out exam certificates; and even if I did, I am sure they would not be widely accredited. There are no percentages, no benchmarks, no instruments, crude or calculating, with which to measure the relative success of your studies. It will not necessarily bolster academic excellence, address a skills deficit or place a premium on the long-term economic value of your intellectual equipment. It won't rubber-stamp you for public glory of any kind.

'If anything it will do the opposite. Walk into your new school tomorrow and start talking about … well, pretty much anything that I have told you, and they may very well send you to a 'special' school after the other kids have ridiculed you and dragged you literally through the mud. If there is no discernible self-enclosed end, then they'll find you the right kind of straitjacket. Everything these days is measurable. And if it can't be measured, it doesn't exist. Which is the more insane? Have *you* been through any test yet? Have you had to sit any exams?"

"No. Not yet."

"Oh well that's re-assuring. Nothing at all?"

"No."

"Do you like your primary school?"

"Yes."

"Well, it's all about to change. At the end of next year, you'll have your first exam. Your first taste of the adult mind."

"Is there *anything* good about getting older?"

"No. Not really."

"Oh. Nothing at all?"

"It's all pretty miserable. But then if the way things seem is incongruous with the way they are, and if misery is a corollary of the way things seem, then recognising that the way things seem is not necessarily the way they are might alleviate the misery."

"Oh right."

"In fact you might say that the misery is a condition of the failure to recognise the incongruity between the way things seem and the way things are. Which *could* mean that everything is, in fact, unconditionally good, if it is considered or imagined from the right perspective."

"Okay."

"On the other hand, if every perspective is at some level necessarily incongruous with a fuller picture of reality, that means the perspective from which everything could be construed as unequivocally good is unthinkable. You see ... a circle never stops."

"Yes ... I can kind of understand."

"But?"

"But ... I don't ... I don't ... know ..."

"You're hesitating ..."

"Yes, I know."

"Don't hesitate; just say what you want to say."

"Every time I come here ... I get nervous. Even if it is about being bitten by snakes or just the sea."

"What snakes?"

"Well, I mean, I get nervous. But every time I come here, at the end of it, I feel better; and even if I get nervous about coming back again, I always want to come back. It's like I can't stop myself. And the things you say ... I don't think I really understand them, but in the end they calm me down. I get quite worked up. But they calm me down."

"This place, these stories, we have stretched out over the last few weeks – they are my refuge. These words ... perhaps they are becoming your refuge too."

"Perhaps. Yes, perhaps they are. Earlier ... when I first arrived, I said that I was worried that you might not be here if I come back next week when I have started at my new school. I know this is a silly thing to think, but I was expecting you would ... I mean, *is* it a silly thing to think?"

"I don't think so."

"Oh."

"You look horrified. Why should it be?"

"Because ... I mean ... well ... I am me and you are you. I guess you live here."

"And the two of us have nothing whatsoever to do with each other?"

"Well, only since the last few weeks."

"But who is to say that I was here *before* the last few weeks? ... What started this line of inquiry anyway?"

"It was just a feeling I suppose. But also ..."

"Yes?"

"The first time I came here the front door of the lighthouse was padlocked. And the second time I came here it was padlocked again; but it was padlocked on the outside while you were on the inside. I know because you waved at me through one of the windows. How could you have done that? How could you have padlocked the door on the outside while you were still inside?"

"It's a conundrum."

"You must have had someone to lock you in. But that person would have had to unlock the padlock to let you out; but no-one came to unlock the padlock. I know. I was there. I was watching."

"It is a paradox."

"And, I mean, you can't live here. You just can't. There's no furniture. There's nothing. The windows are boarded up."

"It is a puzzle."

"Even my mum and dad say that no-one lives in the lighthouse."

"Yes, but they are biased."

"What do you mean?"

"Well, they've been educated. Or I should say, 'educated'. And what do you think an 'educated' person would say about an older man living alone in a lighthouse, expounding their history and meaning to innocent young boys?"

"They would say you are a pervert."

"Yes, maybe even a lunatic pervert."

"Yes, yes."

"You see, you stand on the cusp of your education. Even you can grasp what it is like to think like an adult. And if you follow through the kind of thinking that becomes an adult member of the human race, you also would come to the view that if a man lives in a lighthouse, he must have chosen to live there, and that his life in the lighthouse continues independently of anyone – not just curious young boys at the threshold of their journey into adult life at the end of the twentieth century – who happens to visit him. But this is the kind of thinking that we are calling into question."

"You mean that ..."

"Yes ... go on ..."

"You mean that ... I don't know what to think."

"What were you going to say?"

"You're saying that you don't really live here."

"Yes – that's just what I'm saying. What do you think of that, then?"

"I don't know. It doesn't seem very likely."

"*Of course* it doesn't seem likely."

"You mean you only appear when I appear?"

"Or perhaps it is vice versa."

"You mean, *I* only appear when you appear?"

"Who can say? There is some mischievous act of imagination at work, one way or the other."

"But I never *disappear*. I'm going home this evening. We're having Angel Delight."

"What do you mean you never disappear? You might disappear at any moment. For one thing, I might still turn out to be the lunatic pervert you still think I might be. If I were – and I want to stress that I am not – you would probably disappear very quickly! You see, you are already thinking with the conceit of an adult: you are basing an entire edifice of knowledge on foundations that are fundamentally unstable."

"So if I come back next week, you *won't* be here?"

"Judging by your answers so far, I am in the process of disappearing before your very eyes! Perhaps in a certain sense we both are."

"But I don't want that to happen. Can't I persuade you to stay another week, or perhaps even longer?"

"No. I don't think so. This process is inevitable. Who knows – by the end of next week you may have changed your mind. I know what I think of the education that awaits you, but you are pre-empting your own experience of it. It will try hard to win you over, and I would even hazard a guess that at some point it will win you over. You will be fully initiated."

"So what should I do?"

"There is only one thing you can do."

"What's that?"

"Say goodbye."

"Is that all I can do?"

"I suppose it maybe just an 'au revoir'. But only if you remember these lessons; that's why I think they are important. Because they commit to the memory something important, and no matter how deeply buried in the memory they become, they can always be recalled. If the key points of this lesson are correct, then in some sense we will meet again, but in different roles; perhaps on that occasion you will be the teacher, the lonely recluse, the purveyor of strange tales, and the inventor of lighthouses."

VII

The rain has stopped or receded into the blustery clouds. There is an intermission of faint blue sky. His clothes are now dry, but stiff and crumpled with the residue of rain, though some condensation still drips on the inside of his waterproofs. He is not cycling back along the peninsula in the way that he has done at the end of every other lesson. He wheels his bicycle slowly, head hanging pensively, as he steps along the concrete. His movements suggest that the lighthouse and the peninsula are taking leave of him, rather than the other way around. They suggest that he is just fixed in one spot, as the ground moves beneath him. Considered in this way, he looks like a lacklustre pet mouse treading a play-wheel.

Everything is, as always, quiet on the peninsula. The noises of the harbour, the industrial clamour, the sound of corroded chain scraping against metal, are too distant and easily lost in the wind. The closest sound is the unforced whir of the chain on his bicycle.

He wears his hood down. His hair flies around freely. Occasional grains of sand catch him in the eye.

He is lost in thought. At the end of the three lessons, he is still trying to understand the 'lesson' he is meant to have understood. And to determine whether or not he has understood what he is meant to have understood, he is going over each lesson, trying to recall the details of the story and the man's running commentary.

David wishes he had taken notes or, better still, smuggled a Dictaphone into his pocket, so that he might play their dialogue over and over again, or maybe even transcribe it. He wants to interrogate all the details more closely. He wants to ensure he has left no stone unchecked, so that no furtive beasties of meaning go unnoticed. He even thinks that he would like to turn around once more, and ask a few more questions of the man. He can hear the phrasing in his head: "You know when you said that ... did you mean ...?"; "You told me that when you were a child ... but when you were an adult ... and not a moment ago you said ..."

Even where he can't actually see the contradictions, he can see the logical structures that will allow him to expose them. All he lacks is the detail, which he cannot grasp because there is too much of it, and it is too hard. He doesn't really understand it. It slips through his fingers, like grains of sand finely ground by the aeons.

The lessons are slowly merging into a series of pictures rather than a set of tightly woven syllogisms, premises and conclusions designed to fortify overarching premises and conclusions, which may or may not stand up to scrutiny. Instead, he sees simplistic fragments from the story, scenes peppered with his assumptions. And common motifs seem to leap out at him: in particular, woods and girls' legs.

The countryside around him is mostly open; there are few trees and little in the way of woodland. The valleys up on the moorland contain copses, woods, old broken branches, and gnarled roots, obtruding from riverbanks. But, more locally, the land is exposed, so he is not sure how to place his image of the man as a teenager, trying desperately to placate the fuming of his hot-legged neighbour. He imagines her calves with a certain amount of girth.

But he is losing his way.

"Concentrate!" he mutters under his breath, and grips the handlebars of his bicycle more vigorously.

With each step he takes away from the lighthouse, a detail, or some hold he has on the education he has experienced, escapes him. And is this really all he has taken away from the three journeys out to the lighthouse – a failed attempt to imagine trees and an embryonic fetishisation of the most prehensile part of the female physiology? He shakes his head, full of shame and self-reproach. He can do better than this. And he *must* do better that this. The day is growing late; soon it will be the early evening, then dusk, then bedtime, then he will be damned to his life as an adult. He feels sure that he must understand this lesson before teatime or it will be too late, and he will spend the rest of his life unhappy and alone, working as some minor functionary with no appetite for life, quietly put-upon and derided by his peers, and trapped in a circuit of delusions, which he will lack the courage to doubt.

If he tries harder, he can see the overall aim of the lessons: the move from child to adult and back to child. He thinks he can see that much. But he can only understand it formally, because he has not yet made it beyond the first stage. He is just a child, and his notion of what it means to be an adult is conditioned by his perspective as a child. He thinks that he must first become an adult before he can stand a chance of appreciating the man's lessons. But the man had discouraged this view, and even suggested that David had everything at his disposal without growing a literal or metaphorical inch.

This suggestion taunts and frustrates David, and creates the impression that only a slight re-alignment of perspective, which he cannot quite find, would crystallise his understanding of the matter.

He is only a quarter of the way back towards the mainland, and at this point he stops firmly in his tracks to think the matter through thoroughly. He cannot spare the time, and if he waits until he gets home, he knows that something will stand in the way, or he will find a spurious excuse to avoid thinking about it. So, he lodges himself firmly in the middle of the road, and decides that he will only drag his heels back to his house once he has made some progress.

He realises quickly that there are different ways in which he can approach the issue: he could keep working on his memory, trying to recall all the details from the last few weeks in the hope that a few loose pebbles plucked judiciously might set in motion a landslide of recollection; but the vagueness and incompetence of his memory is too stubborn. He can, alternatively, hypothesize about what it might be like to be an adult, and try to dovetail that speculation with the imperfect understanding he already has.

Imagining life as an adult is no easy task, despite plenty of material with which to work. For one thing, adults seem to be quite different. The man he knows who lives in the caravan park, and who managed to mostly avoid flying planes during the Second World War, is gentle, unassuming, and has a distant look, as though the mechanism that keeps his stare fixed on the material world might easily vacate its post and leave his eyeballs rolling inanely in their sockets. The cigarette-smelling man with a tattoo who taught him to swim at the municipal swimming baths (and who coincidentally had also been in the services) has a different pair of eyes. His are predatory, full of practical goals and short-term victories. Both sets of eyes reinforce David's firmly held belief that most adults escape insanity by only the slenderest of margins.

But rather than become mired in the endless differences, he thinks it would be better to start from some of things that adults have in common (though not their poor mental health).

He begins with height. All children look up – except to things like ladybirds, ants, babies and particularly small children. Whereas, for adults, most of things that affect their immediate attention appear beneath the crowns of their heads. (There are exceptions, but there are exceptions to every general rule.) This downward outlook on things must, he thinks, be significant. There must be some clue here.

If, most of the time, adults are distracted by objects that appear beneath their heads, then, he reasons, that there must be an awful lot of things that they don't see. Children, on the other hand, are looking upwards for most of the time. This means that they not only see the clunking giants that stomp about above them, but the endless sky. Adults probably don't pay much attention to the branches of trees, hot air balloons, and double-decker buses; but for a child these things stand out, and become a part of ...

"No, no, that can't be it" he says, bashing his handlebars.

He is thinking like a child. These are just simple observations, the sort of thing that learned men of the Middle Ages would have counted as pedestrian intelligence, but which, to the sophistication of the modern age, looks idiotic. Analysis is missing from his thoughts. At the moment his mind is just bumping into the material world, and any apparent sense that he manages to make out of it is purely incidental.

Analysis. The word comes back to him and rattles around his head, trying to incite the redundant matter of his mind to achieve something close to its meaning. But his mind seems to oppose its meaning, and the cells of his brain are hanging out in churlish factions, like late adolescents urinating in a public bus shelter. If he could step inside his mind, he would give them a talking to.

David half wonders what it might be like to encounter one of his brain cells face to face. He has an impression of an amorphous, deformed, mollusc-like creature with puffy eyes, making quick-fire snide comments in-between guzzling from a family-sized tub of chicken nuggets. He wants to drag the slimy anti-social creature into the lighthouse and say to the man, "Look, this is one of my brain cells; you see what I have to work with!"

If he really shakes his head around, he might be able to destroy the hideous creatures inside his head, break them up and reduce them to a pulpy mash, which would dribble out of his head through his ears, and leave room for something solid, noble and cultured to grow in its place. Moshing is the undiscovered answer to his problems.

And yet in spite of these problems, David still finds himself daring to come to terms with the things the man has told him. The point that has been impressed upon him is that he must remember his life as a child; he must not get lost in the hazy conflation of disorganised memories, dreams and imaginary phantasms that roam freely around his mind. This time in his life, the man seems to be saying, is something to which he must return, something he must be able to recall from his memory when he needs it. He must be able to look back to ensure the entire landscape of his adult life is not governed by a single perspective. He might, that is to say, find himself wanting to imagine his life as a child again. Like the man's story, and like the lighthouse (and if the man is to be believed, like the man himself), David might turn his own childhood into a park for the exercise of his imagination.

Something suddenly clicks into place. If he is remembering his own ignorance in order to appreciate later in life that his maturity is really besieged, beleaguered, and full of pointless pretensions, then that means he has nothing really to worry about. If he is just moving between differing degrees of ignorance, then does his current ignorance matter too much? It is, after all, only proportionate to the conditions of his life as a child. His idiotic rambling will only be superseded by a different kind of idiotic rambling, albeit one that is institutionalised, governed by laws, constitutions, and rolling coverage in the modern media.

David does not, of course, think these exact thoughts, but only an approximation to them, perhaps born from a need to come away from his journeys out to the lighthouse with something to show for it. He may not have worked out all the details, or discovered all the angles of interpretation, but the beam of the lighthouse has temporarily scanned the horizons of his brain. Or so he thinks.

He wheels his bicycle back towards the mainland. One or two drops of rain have already reached him, and, to his right, a tempestuous explosion of rage is working up a fury. David surveys the rain clouds, the peninsula, the choppy waters, and the largely featureless landscape. Little to no wildlife is visible, though he knows the peninsula contains plenty of it. All the creatures are clinging desperately to the land, hiding away in the grasses, burrowing in the sand, taking refuge behind a piece of driftwood, which creates the false impression that the bad weather has swept the world clean. And where a creature dares to emerge, it looks lonely, out of place, and suffocated by the stretch of land and murky water that surrounds it. There is even a sense that if a creature left itself too exposed it might be swept out to sea, or carried up into the rioting vault of the sky by a cyclonic blast of wind.

David grips his bicycle. He thinks that if he rides his bicycle, a particularly fierce gust of wind might carry him away, and his only hope would be to cycle precariously on the currents of the wind until he can find a way back to earth. But by that stage who knows where the whims of nature might have taken him.

Carried here, carried there, he pictures himself looking down on the world, and its different cities and cultures, hoping to land in a place where people have things like chocolate and freshly baked bread. He doesn't think he could hack it in a more survivalist culture. They would turn *him* into freshly baked bread, and mop up his intestines like baked beans.

In which case, he might be better off just riding the skies, day after day, night after night, pedalling forever between the sun, the moon and the darkness in-between. But any appeal this might have would soon wear off; and it is for these reasons that he sticks firmly to the view that he must walk back along the peninsula.

How much time he has now spent assailed by the unpredictable journeys of his brain, he really doesn't know.

"Concentrate," he says again. "I must learn to concentrate."

But then, he thinks, perhaps not.

www.ingramcontent.com/pod-product-compliance
Lightning Source LLC
LaVergne TN
LVHW041635060526
838200LV00040B/1582